MW00988278

With the tour group's attention focused over there as they strained to hear ghostly music, I had the opportunity to look down at Maggie.

The knot in my stomach twisted, my gut clenching around it.

Maggie looked back up at me, tears in her big brown eyes. She shook her head, sadness and confusion warring in her expression.

Then she looked back towards the mausoleum, curling her fingers in a wave. She made no sound, but I clearly understand the words her lips formed.

"Bye-bye."

Despite the unfettered sun baking down on me, I felt a chill shudder through me.

Aaron, who loved the Hollywood Forever Cemetery so much he kept showing up for work every day after he was dead, had shuffled off this mortal coil.

He was gone.

Really gone.

GHOSTED

NIKKI ASHBURNE – BOOK 1

DAYLE A. DERMATIS

SOUL'S
ROAD
PRESS

GHOSTED
Nikki Ashburne – Book 1
Dayle A. Dermatis

Print edition published 2018 by Soul's Road Press

Copyright © Dayle A. Dermatis. All rights reserved, including the right of reproduction, in whole or in part in any form, without written permission of the publisher, except in the case of brief quotations embedded in critical articles and reviews.

This is a work of fiction. Names, characters, places, and events are either the product of the author's imagination or are used fictitiously, and any resemblance to actual persons, living or dead, business establishments, events, or locales is entirely coincidental.

ISBN-13: 978-1-946462-07-7 (trade paperback)
ISBN-10: 1-946462-07-1 (trade paperback)

Inquiries should be addressed to
Soul's Road Press
info@soulsroadpress.com
http://www.soulsroadpress.com

Cover design by Melody Simmons
Soul's Road Press logo: Designs by Trapdoor

For Kris,
because she kept asking,
"Is the Nikki book done? I love Nikki. When can I read it?"

GHOSTED

ONE

WHAT WOULD you do if your friends started disappearing, and you didn't know how to stop it?

What if all of those friends were ghosts?

Dude, if you'd asked me that a year ago, I would've told you that was a great pitch line, but my father's the movie producer, not me. I wouldn't have thought you were serious, and if you were, I would've laughed so hard my tequila sunrise would've shot right out of my nose.

Then it happened to me. And nobody's laughing.

YOU KNOW HOW IN MOVIES, someone will be at a loud party, but they seem to be in a bubble where the sound barely filters through? That was how I felt right now. Around me, people laughed and talked, house music pounded, but it was all...distant.

I moved slowly, making no sudden movements so I didn't break the sphere, which I imagined was thin like a soap bubble, completely invisible.

I still wore the stylish black dress I'd worn earlier today to the funeral; I hadn't wanted to go all the way home to change, although I'd taken off the little hat with the attached veil. No normal twenty-something owns hats like that, but I'd worn it when I played Mourner #5 in one of my father's scream flicks, and I'd kept it, because it was cute. Wardrobe never noticed.

I think my *abuelita*, Grandma Rosa, would have liked it.

I'd left directly from the graveside service to come to the party because I needed the familiar, my comfort zone. But everything felt wrong, different.

I felt different.

Drink in hand, I moved through the crowd, half-seen. It wasn't my first drink of the evening. Gin and tonics, that's what I was drinking this week, because I'd noticed they were what Evan Frohman was drinking, and maybe we could bond over them. After that, I could ease back to drinking things that didn't taste like tree vomit.

We were in a trendy, modern house in the Hollywood Hills—I had no idea who owned it—one that used to be chrome and glass but now, after renovation, was some odd combination of shabby-chic French with Asian accents, and faux-rustic, grey-weathered boards on the walls with painted inspirations like "Breathe" and "Live." On the other hand, the deck, which overlooked the glittering lights of Tinseltown, *was* all glass, to give a dizzying illusion of being suspended in midair.

Wile E. Coyote, I am not. But I could appreciate that the view was spectacular, even as I clutched the nearly invisible edge of the railing with one hand.

My name is Nikki Ashburne. Yes, the daughter of Edward Ashburne, mega-producer, king of the teen sex comedy, sultan of the revival of nighttime soaps. And this (imagine me sweeping my hand over the midnight vista) is my playground.

Yep, I was definitely getting tipsy. Not drunk—not yet—but tonight, unusually, I was steadily working on it.

Even out here, the air clogged with pricy perfume and aftershave. Even out here, I couldn't seem to drag in a full, clean breath of air. Smog wasn't the problem; affluence was.

I raised my glass to that.

Voices invaded my bubble.

"No, she definitely had a nose job. That whole thing about losing baby fat in your cheeks so your nose looks slimmer is bullshit. I know, because I got a nose job for my eighteenth birthday."

"Seriously. Why not just admit it? Almost everybody gets something done for graduation."

"Did you hear about Missy? Another DUI. They're talking about rehab."

"Well, she has *got* to learn to hold her phone lower when she's texting, because then the cops don't see it."

"...sex tape..."

"Who calls them *tapes* anymore? Shit, Becca, you sound like my mother..."

A jumble of voices, but I recognized them all: my peeps. Chris, Eden, Jessica, Samantha, Kayla. They tumbled onto the deck in a flurry of glitter, fashion, and sky-high heels.

"There you are," Eden said, flipping her long blond hair over her shoulder in a motion I'd watched her practice in the mirror. "We've been looking for you *everywhere*."

"Sorry," I said before I could stop myself. "Just not in the mood to tear down someone just because they made a bad choice."

"What is *up* with you tonight?" Jessica asked.

"My grandmother died, remember? Today was her

funeral." I felt disconnected as I said it, as if it had happened to someone else. As if I were (freely admitted) a less-than-stellar actress reciting her lines.

Even as I felt disconnected, I knew it was wrong. I was aching—no, it was a sharp pain. Stabbity stabbity in my gut. I downed my drink. I tried to set the highball glass on the balcony, but there was no real balcony, and the glass toppled down to the scrub below.

If anybody noticed, they didn't comment. Or, probably, care. Wasn't their glass.

Although I'd probably be a story later. Pity, I wasn't even all that drunk.

I'm never going to whine about how awful my life is, but the fact is, it's not easy growing up in the public eye. Everything I did was credited to my father paving the way— certainly *I* wasn't pretty enough or talented enough or smart enough. Daddy and I get along great, but he's Edward Ashburne, for crying out loud, which means he's *busy*. And my mother...oh, I did not want to think about my mother right now. I'm not saying she never loved me, but I had been a useful accessory until I got old enough to disagree with her, and then old enough to put her own admitted age in question.

So I'd spent a lot of time with Grandma Rosa, Daddy's mom, over the years. She had her own house on the estate, and even set up a bedroom for me there, and she'd taught me how to make tortillas and read lines with me and told me that I was pretty and talented and most importantly smart enough.

Now she was dead, and I didn't know where to turn. She'd given the best hugs, and I wanted one of them, and I couldn't feel her smooshing me against her ever again.

"Oh, honey, I'm so sorry," Chris said, hugging me. It was

a sincere hug as embraces go, but she still made sure not to smudge her makeup.

Chris Yeates, my best friend, my partner in crime, etc. Stunning blond (via a stunning hairdresser) with curves (some of which were financed), star of the reality show *Young and In Love* (although everyone, including Chris, knew that her "in love" was gay, albeit a great friend). She'd been bugging me to do a cameo on the show.

Maybe next week.

Unless they were filming tonight and I'd have a release form shoved in my face on the way out.

They all swarmed me now, each trying to outdo the others with her false sympathy—even, on the periphery, Asia McBride, who was practically a nobody, a wannabe. How had she even been invited here?

A flurry of sympathy: so sorry, oh darling, hugz, sweetie, what can we do.

"Thanks," I said, blinking back tears. "The funeral was hard..."

I realized my mistake as they went blank. They were sympathetic, but not to the point that I was allowed to bring down the party atmosphere. They'd done their duty—wasn't that enough? Why was I still going on about it?

My grandmother was dead, and all my friends needed everything to be normal.

"Thanks," I repeated, flashing the winning smile I'd learned when my mother entered me in those awful pageants. I mimed shaking an empty glass, since mine had flung itself to its doom. "Let me get a refill, and then you can tell me all about Missy—did she do a duck face for the mug shot again?"

My bubble and I drifted back through the house, through the cigarette and pot smoke, the throb of bass, past

Evan who was doing one-armed pushups, surrounded by a throng of admirers.

This time, I asked for a double shot of tequila, which the bartender provided because bartenders at these types of parties are paid not to ask questions or spill to the press afterwards.

I downed it in three gulps, which burned like hell but made me feel badass for three-tenths of a second. I blinked rapidly to avoid messing up my mascara.

I got another G&T, because I needed something in my hand. I started back for the balcony, but I just didn't have the energy to put on the face they wanted to see.

Evan was now standing on a coffee table for some reason. I saluted him with my drink, and he winked.

I didn't have the energy to do more than flash a smile, but when I felt better...

The pain rolled through me, fresh as a thousand paper cuts splashed with lime juice and salt. How could I ever feel better? How could that be *possible*?

That's when I saw them. No, not ghosts—that would come later. Although these, and this choice I was about to make, would forever haunt me.

The pretty crystal bowl of pills, pink and blue and yellow like cheap candy from a piñata. Candy that offered way more than a sugar rush.

I'd never done drugs. Never really considered it; despite tonight's chase-the-pain-away efforts, I wasn't even that much of a drinker beyond a few social glasses.

My bubble seemed to increase in strength; the world, the party, the people all seemed more distant. I looked around. No one was watching me—but that's not why I looked. I wasn't feeling guilty, and I was certainly far from the first person here to indulge. In very great hindsight, I

GHOSTED   9

think I was looking for someone to break the bubble, to connect with me. But I was alone. Hurting and alone.

And this seemed like the only way to numb the pain. Couldn't make it worse, right?

I have no idea what I chose. I just sort of grabbed two, slid them down my throat with a sip of fizzy pine sap.

I went back out on the deck, already feeling numb from the tequila, and rejoined my friends, smiling and dropping random comments when I was expected to.

And then I started to feel awful. Not just alcohol-spinning awful—I knew this was worse. I knew I'd fucked up, badly, and the horror that comes with that knowledge washed through me. Blackness swarmed at the edge of my sight, and for the second time that night, I dropped my drink. Someone must've realized what was going on because I heard shouts about calling 911 and then everyone was swarming again and I was heading for lights-out.

Well, shit.

Kids, don't try this at home.

THERE'S a lot I don't remember. I have no memory of the ambulance ride, which sucks because I would've liked to have experienced the siren. Is it like on TV? Maybe I'll never know.

I don't remember the ER, which is probably a good thing. Well, I have a vague sense that there was some shouting, and sharp smells, and I'm guessing they stuck tubes down my throat, but who wants to remember that?

This is what I remember: somebody pinching my arm, and then waking up in a room that would have been quiet except for some infernal machine making a pinging noise and some other machine humming.

It was worse than a hangover. My tongue felt fuzzy and my mouth was coated with some thick goo that tasted like battery acid. I reached for water and that made my arm pinch more, so I reluctantly opened my eyes.

I did not know that acoustic tile ceiling.

Everything came into focus slowly, including my brain. I took in the IV—the source of the pinching—the whiteboard on the wall across from the foot of my bed with the date and time and "your nurse's name is Jeannie"; the annoying puffs of air in my nose that turned out to be an oxygen feed; the streaking sunbeams that made me squint.

I felt kinda floaty, and yet my head hurt, which seemed unfair.

I'd learn later that I had a *very* nice private room in a wing of the hospital most people don't even know about. The rich-and-famous wing. The spare-no-expenses wing.

Even though my bed was propped up a bit, it took me several tries to struggle into something resembling a seated position. There was a pitcher of water and a Styrofoam cup and a straw on a rolling tray table, but they were way beyond my abilities to reach, much less hold on to.

"Hello?" Well, I *tried* to say it. I mostly kind of croaked through my Death Valley of a mouth.

The money-has-no-object wing doesn't include a nurse who can't take potty breaks, apparently.

I was looking around for some sort of call button—slowly, because if I turned my head too fast, the room went all spinny, but in a slow-motion kind of way that still made me want to hurl—when I realized there was, in fact, someone in the room with me.

Someone who hadn't been there a moment ago, and who hadn't come in the door.

My *abuelita*, my beloved grandmother—the grandmother whose funeral I had recently attended (How long ago was that? How long had I been here?)—was sitting on the bed.

It was the drugs. Had to be. Making me hallucinate.

She was the same fireplug of a woman I'd seen buried, wearing the royal blue suit she'd had on when she died, with the gold peacock brooch with precious gems in the tail that she'd loved so much—the first major purchase my father had made after his first movie that made it big—pinned on the lapel. (My mother had thrown a royal fit when she'd learned Grandma wanted to be buried with it. I'm surprised she hadn't figured out a way to sneak into the funeral home and replace it with a fake. As if my mother's jewelry wasn't all a gazillion times more expensive.)

It was my grandmother, all right, her skin tanned and wrinkled, her hair as black as the last day she'd dyed it, her dark eyes flashing like they did when she beat me at Rummikub *again*.

Only that wasn't teasing, affectionate triumph in her gaze.

No, her expression was dead clear (pardon the pun): she was *royally pissed off*.

I tried to say something, but the lack of saliva tripped me up again.

It probably wouldn't've helped.

Because my grandmother said, "Nikki Elizabeth Ashburne, how could you be so *stupid*?"

Her palm cracked against my cheek. The sting of it slapped through my prescription-drug floatiness, and I sucked in my breath.

"Don't you *ever* do something like that again!" Grandma Rosa hissed, and then she was gone.

Just, *poof*, gone.

I might've been able to explain it away as a hallucination if my mother hadn't walked in right then, seen the handprint on my face, and raised holy hell. Shrieking was involved. Lawsuits were threatened. Mayhem ensued.

In the quiet center of the vortex, finally sipping some blessed cool water through a bendy straw, I accepted the truth. My life was no longer what it had been.

I could see ghosts.

TWO

BALANCING A TRAY OF TINY, berry-topped tarts, my keys, and my phone, I leaned my shoulder hard against the fire door from the alley to the kitchen of the Ballington Hotel. The door was heavy, and stuck in one corner—yet another thing I had to add to my infinite To Fix list.

The door finally gave way, and I stumbled from the glaringly bright heat of Los Angeles to a cool, dim interior. I couldn't afford to air condition the entire hotel, but a window unit and fans kept the kitchen below scorching.

I was greeted with "Relax" so loud it made my teeth vibrate. The door started to slip shut, and I threw my weight against it just in time.

"Curtis!" I shouted. "Music *off*!"

Frankie Goes to Hollywood was silenced in mid "ow." Distantly I heard Curtis mutter "Sorry," and then Janie murmured "Thank *God*" with a sigh of relief.

I sighed with relief, too, because I knew the neighbors hadn't heard. Nobody could hear the music but me.

And the otherworldly residents of the fabulous Art Deco Ballington Hotel, formerly home to Hollywood's elite.

Because the hotel wasn't open for business, the vast kitchen was mostly unused. What did I need with an eight-burner gas stove, four ovens, and a griddle the size of Catalina Island? I kept everything clean, but mostly just used a cutting board, a few pieces of cutlery, and the big sink—because fine china and silver couldn't be run through a dishwasher.

For myself, I mostly ate takeout.

The original walk-in fridge and freezer with slatted wooden shelves and industrial door with a heavy clunking latch wasn't turned on. I'd hauled a normal fridge in, which was enough for the clotted cream and lemon curd and sandwich fixings—cucumber and cream cheese, curried chicken, egg and cress, and of course cheddar and Branston pickle.

I'd developed an unhealthy obsession with cheddar and Branston pickle, which is why it was Solange's job to make the sandwiches.

This is what my life has become.

Sometimes people say to me, "Does anybody ever tell you that you look like Nikki Ashburne?"

Usually I answer with, "Isn't she dead?"

I've always been one for honesty, you know? A lot of people do think that I died. Point of fact is, I did, for about a minute and a half. I didn't see any white light or tunnel with loved ones waiting for me, and apparently that's a big crock of shit anyway.

We all know what happened when I woke up.

Other times, people just say, "You look familiar...are you someone famous?"

I don't exactly know how to respond to that one.

I guess I really look different without the extensions and the heavy makeup, and wearing more clothes than would cover a Barbie Doll. I don't bother having my hair straightened anymore, either, and I've let it go back to its natural reddish blond rather than the lavender I'd favored then to set myself apart from all the bottle blonds, and curly. I keep it in a terribly unfashionable 1920s-inspired bob, longer in the front, which looks great on me, I think.

Am I famous? A year ago, I would have said yes, no question. I was routinely on the cover of the tabloids, usually in the company of another starlet or barely legal actress or someone otherwise known-for-being-known, on our way to or coming out of some club. The party girls, they called us. Celebutantes.

Back then I'd called myself an actress, but I wasn't, not really. The only roles I'd had were ones I'd wheedled my father into giving me.

How I made my money then was by being paid to be seen—at movie premieres, at club openings, at trendy restaurants, even at charity events. I dabbled at having my own perfume, played around with designing hats, even recorded a demo. (The less said about the latter, the better. It's buried in a vault somewhere. Someday I'll find it and give it a ritual burning...)

Now...

Now I own a derelict 1920s hotel that nobody stays in, and give ghost tours of Hollywood.

The ghosts of Hollywood are kind enough to help me out with that.

As for the hotel, Grandma Rosa had loved home reno shows, which of course I'd watched with her, and clearly they'd damaged my brain.

I lived here, too. I kinda loved this damn place. Okay, really loved it. I'd had no idea I loved old buildings until now, and I just wanted to hug this one.

Twelve floors of Art Deco goodness, although all I'd

been able to fix so far were a third-floor suite of my own and most of the ground floor: kitchen, dining room, lobby, parlor, solarium. I was especially fond of the solarium.

Now I slid the black plastic tray onto the enormous stainless-steel-topped prep island before all the tarts slid to one end and piled up against the clear plastic cover. The bakery gave me a discount for regular orders as well as including their business cards in the packets of materials I gave my tour groups. Win-win, right there.

It was a testament to my constitution that I hadn't been popping those delectable confections into my mouth all the way from the bakery. But they weren't for me, and all I could do was hope for leftovers.

(That little lime curd one decorated with strawberry slices and blackberries and a decorative swirl of fresh whipped cream? Maybe I'd hide it in the back of the fridge.)

I did a quick check to make sure everything else was in order for when Solange arrived: bread and sandwich ingredients, tea dishes and silver washed and on the cart, various china teapots ready to be filled with tea and boiling water.

I don't know why I'd decided high tea at an old hotel was the proper cap to an afternoon of visiting the haunted sites of Hollywood, but the tourists seemed to like it, and it let me indulge in the leftovers. The tour business didn't bring in swaths of money the way attending parties and doing reality shows had, and much of the income went to working on the Ballington.

I glanced at the time on my phone and winced.

"Tour group this afternoon," I called out. "Remember to look alive, people."

Somebody—Curtis, probably—gave me a razzberry.

Because everyone I was talking to was dead.

Sometimes I crack myself up.

There were a lot of things I didn't understand about ghosts. How Curtis—a friend of the Coreys, who died in the late 1980s when his car went off a Mulholland Drive cliff—could play music (at *any* volume) when there was no stereo in the entire place, or how he'd heard me when he wasn't in the kitchen.

I didn't have time to think about that now. I was running so very la—

The kitchen door opened again, with the same hitch from the sticking corner. Unlike me, my friend Solange entered serenely and gracefully.

Solange was tall, with mahogany skin so smooth and nonporous, it could make cosmetic manufacturers weep. She looked like a Voudon queen, and indeed had descended from one (not Marie Laveau, she says, but someone similar whose name I can never remember). With her strong features and fierce dark eyes, she's mesmerizing. Her voice was soft and yet somehow compellingly powerful, with a Creole lilt that gets more pronounced when she's impassioned or entranced.

Solange was my best friend—my best living friend, that is. Okay, pretty much my only living friend, which would be pathetic if I didn't have so many dead friends. (Solange, like the dead, didn't judge like the Hollywood elite did.) Except for my brother, who didn't believe me, and a tiny handful of other people, she was pretty much the only living person who knew I could see ghosts.

She had a different relationship with the dead—she couldn't see them the same way I could, as almost-alive but with a slight Spidey-sense tingle that told me otherwise. Sometimes I even didn't realize someone was a ghost right away.

That was usually awkward.

Solange's dark eyes widened when she saw me. "*Cher*," she said in her smooth New Orleans accent, "what are you doing here? Don't you have a group to pick up?"

She put down the various bags she was carrying and enveloped me in a hug. I inhaled her unique scent, something dark and musky that reminded me of New Orleans, even though I've never been there.

"Yes, and I'm late, thanks to my mother," I said. "I'll explain later. I prepped the others last night. Gotta go—see you at the usual time." I tucked my phone in my pocket and dashed back out the door. It hadn't closed all the way, so I didn't have to fight with it. Small victories.

The hot, dry air hit me like a slap. Don't let those imported palm trees fool you—Los Angeles is a desert, plain and simple.

At the other end of the alley that runs between the Ballington's service door and the building next door, I saw movement. Ah, Donny.

Donny's my personal paparazzi/stalker. He's not like the other paps; at least, not as far as I've seen. In fact, I kinda like Donny.

For one thing, he has a special place in my heart because he actually sent me a sympathy card after my grandmother died. With a personal, handwritten note inside. A big step up from how my now-former friends had handled the situation.

Anyway, I've actually talked to Donny a few times, and he's a reasonable guy. Good with a camera, too, honestly—I'm not just saying that because he's taken actually flattering pictures of me in the past. He really does have a way with it.

He's got white-boy dreads that don't look entirely stupid on him, some nice muscles, a tattoo of a raven on his biceps.

Donny's dream is to be a crime-scene photographer.

Unfortunately, he had some run-ins with the law in his day —mostly minor stuff, like car theft and vandalism. No violence, no murder, but a couple of the offenses came just after his eighteenth birthday, so they're still on his open record.

That means his chances of getting hired by the police are just about nil.

He could make a lot more money doing fashion photography, but he says he's not interested. Pap work gives him the adrenaline rush he's looking for, the thrill of the chase. I guess there's a certain amount of detective work in it, too, figuring out where a celebrity's going to be.

Not that my movements are hard to figure out these days.

At any rate, he's not a bad guy, doesn't get in my face. A girl could have a worse stalker. So, as usual, I gave him a friendly wave as I hit the remote to unlock my van (hey, I ferry tourists around—I really *do* need a monster honkin' SUV).

He doesn't get a lot of pictures of me that come out clearly. You know how ghosts show up all wonky on film? Blurry smudges, or a swirl of lights, or random splotches? My frequent proximity to ghosts means that extends to me.

I opened the van door, pausing just for a few seconds for Maggie to clamber up before I climbed into the driver's seat. I hate the feeling of a ghost passing through me. For one thing, it's like a blast of air conditioning—from the inside. Painfully cold.

I'm a (former) celebrity; I'm used to having my personal space violated. But this is entirely different from having hordes of people crowded around you, wanting a piece of you.

This is someone—something—*sharing* that personal space with you for a moment. Shudder.

Maggie's another ghost, obviously. I don't know too much about her, because she can't, or won't, talk. I know she was six when she died, because she held up her fingers when I asked. She has brown Shirley Temple ringlets and big brown eyes with the longest lashes you've ever seen outside of a '60s makeup shoot.

I don't know how she died, and honestly, I don't think I want to. She's too little, and the very idea just creeps me out. She had just shown up when I'd been jogging in Griffith Park. I'd seen her, but hadn't realized she was following me until I got back to my car and she just hopped in next to me. That had been almost a year ago.

I also don't know why she chose me, but we're pretty much attached at the hip. Maybe because I'm the first living person to notice her. I think she just needed someone. As had I—there had been paparazzi around my car when I'd gotten there, eager for a rare sighting of Nikki Ashburne so soon after her sojourn from the rehab-cum-spa. Yet those pictures never showed up on the tabloid sites, and I realized only much later that that had been because of my new friend.

Because she's always next to me, it's impossible for anyone to get a clear picture of me. Like I said, I don't get many paparazzi after me anymore, other than Donny, but it's kind of restful knowing I don't really have to worry about it.

"Party time," I said to Maggie, reversing the SUV out of the alley. I had to go around the block because they had the street torn up at the intersection.

She looked at me solemnly and patted my leg—well, patted the air near my thigh. Chilly.

If anyone had told me a year ago what a weird life I'd end up with, I would have directed them straight to my therapist.

If anyone had told me how hard I'd fight to keep this weird life...

THREE

I PICKED up the tour group around the corner from Grauman's Chinese Theatre—itself allegedly haunted by actor Victor Kilian, searching for his killer.

I'd had to look up Victor Kilian on imdb.com. Turns out he was murdered by burglars at his home. So why would he be hanging out at the theatre? Did he think they were going to steal some cement footprints next?

But the stories make my job easier. I can whip the tourists into a frightener's frenzy with a bunch of random tales, so by the time we're at the hotel, they're ready for a real paranormal experience.

Which my friends cheerfully provide.

The traffic gods favored me, and I arrived five minutes early. I stuck my sign on the back window, kept the AC running, and pulled out my phone to check my e-mail.

First, and unsurprisingly, my mother's personal assistant Susie, reminding me that I was expected at the house at two tomorrow to prep for the *Day into Knight* premiere. Yes, I knew that, and yes, it was on my calendar, but I could hear my mother's voice asking Susie to make sure I knew *even though we'd talked about it earlier today*.

Then, someone wanting to include me in a Where Are They Now? type show. *What?* It's been a *year*. It's not as if I'd been at the pinnacle of a fabulous career ten years ago and chucked it all to raise Burmese goats in Eugene, Oregon.

There was also yet another message from some amateur ghost hunter who wanted to camp out in my hotel for the weekend with all his equipment. I'd already told him three times he was welcome to book a tour, but I didn't do private visits like that. Since this was his fifth message, I deleted the e-mail unanswered.

And then the group arrived: eight people, an extended family from Iowa. Mom, dad, and two kids, plus a brother and sister-in-law and their kid, and another sister.

Kids are weird. (In a lot of ways, yes, but I'm being specific here.) For a good chunk of their early lives, they're open to just about anything. They see ghosts—and/or faeries, boggarts, the Boogeyman, their stuffed animals talking to them, whatever—and they're okay with that. At some point that just goes away (which is pretty sad, I think).

My tour can be very different if there's an open-and-willing kid on board. There are two other basic modes they can be in: one, they get entirely freaked out by the whole thing (which is why I suggest nobody younger than eight), or two, they're bored shitless and think the entire thing is bogus, or whatever kids these days say.

Sometimes I ask my ghosts to ramp it up for the latter kids, just to see them lose it. Hee.

One of today's kids was eight or nine, I guessed, and he stared at me as he clambered into his seat. Or was he staring near me, and looking at Maggie? He didn't say anything, but I wondered.

Then again, he was wearing a top hat with Mickey Mouse ears. It could just be his way.

The Iowans were grateful for the air conditioning in the SUV, as well as for the chilled bottled water I handed out, gratis.

"Hi, I'm Nikki of Hollywood Hauntings," I said through my headset once they were all buckled in. "How're we all doing today?"

A chorus of "good" and "fine" and one lone, wistful "are we going to have ice cream?" Thankfully there was no "I gotta pee."

"Did you all check out Mann's Chinese Theatre?" A chorus of yes's. "Before we get going, I just wanted to mention that Mann's is reportedly haunted by the ghost of Victor Kilian. Did anyone see him?"

"Who?" one of the moms asked.

And we were off. Yeehaw.

I drove up near the Hollywood sign (you can't drive all the way to it, but you can get close enough for a good view and photo op) and told them about suicide jumper Peg Entwistle in the 1930s, and how her presence is accompanied by the overpowering scent of gardenias.

It's always a bitch getting the van turned around and back down the narrow, twisting road. Although it's paved and crammed with the houses of minor celebrities and directors and whoever, the street is as narrow and switchbacked as an Alpine goat track. We were decidedly bigger than a goat, and had the added challenge of an obstacle course thanks to the trash and recycle bins along the curb.

Then we swung back down to the Roosevelt Hotel, where I took them to the mirror near the elevators where

Marilyn Monroe has been spotted. Marilyn Monroe died in her home, although she'd lived in the hotel for two years earlier in her career, and the mirror had been in her suite.

Fact was, the ghost haunting the Roosevelt was a Marilyn Monroe *impersonator*; a mediocre one who didn't get a lot of notice. But after her death, she wandered through the Roosevelt Hotel and everyone went apeshit. She's more famous dead than she was alive, and she milks that for all she's worth.

She was a friend, and she flickered a little in the corner of the mirror for the tour group. As most groups did, they decided it was a special effect that the hotel had installed.

I told them about Montgomery Clift and the other ghosts that reportedly haunted the Roosevelt (although Marilyn was the only one I knew to be fact), and then we were on to our next stop: the Hollywood Forever Cemetery. Home to a whole lot of famous dead people and at least one decidedly nonfamous ghost.

It's a pretty place, with outdoor gravestones and a couple of vast indoor mausoleums, and even a small lake. I drove slowly around the curving roads, nattering about the various grave sites, and parked on Maple Avenue between the lake and the small white marble mausoleum. Luckily, there were no funerals today. Nothing killed a ghost tour like an actual dead person.

We poured out of the SUV. A couple of the kids wandered over to Douglas Fairbanks' grave, because his has a spiffy water feature. I stood in the shade of the Cathedral Mausoleum, one of the big ones, keeping an eye out for Aaron so I could give him the surreptitious hand signal to indicate the level of haunting for today.

Aaron Schwabach had been a caretaker here. I'm not sure exactly when, but I know it was for a long time, because he's one ancient guy. Apparently he worked right up 'til the day he died, stoop-shouldered and grey and a little slow, because he loved the place so much. He died peacefully in his sleep, but he hangs out here to keep an eye on the new groundskeepers and make sure nobody's messing up his hard work.

You've got to respect that kind of dedication. Who loves their job that much nowadays?

Aaron thinks my tour shtick is hilarious, but more importantly, he thinks my clients are respectful people, not hooligans intent on tearing up the place or bothering the myriad of ducks and geese and swans that use the mani-cured lawns as their personal toilet. Since he was always on the alert, I didn't have to prep him; I just showed up, he got the signal, and then he'd throw some rocks into the lake or whack a rake against a headstone or whatever was needed.

Today, though, Aaron was nowhere to be seen—by any of us.

I frowned. This was so not like Aaron.

I started my spiel, hoping he would show up, but a strange knot in the pit of my stomach was telling me other-wise. My spiel was pretty lame, I have to say, without him actually doing something.

Wait...I had Maggie with me. Maybe she could throw some rocks or scatter some flowers.

But how could I ask her with the tour group standing right here? It wasn't as if I could shout "Look! A moose!" and point in the opposite direction to distract them. (They probably wouldn't care. There are moose in Iowa, right? God, my geography stinks.)

On a whim, I pointed out Johnny Ramone's grave nearby, topped with a statue of Mr. Ramone himself wielding a guitar (of course). "Sometimes," I said, pitching my voice conspiratorially so they had to lean in to hear me, "they say, if you listen hard enough, you can hear Johnny playing his guitar..."

With their attention focused over there as they strained to hear ghostly music, I had the opportunity to look down at Maggie.

The knot in my stomach twisted, my gut clenching around it.

Maggie looked back up at me, tears in her big brown eyes. She shook her head, sadness and confusion warring in her expression.

Then she looked back towards the mausoleum, curling her fingers in a wave. She made no sound, but I clearly understand the words her lips formed.

"Bye-bye."

Despite the unfettered sun baking down on me, I felt a chill shudder through me.

Aaron, who loved the Hollywood Forever Cemetery so much he kept showing up for work every day after he was dead, had shuffled off this mortal coil.

He was gone.

Really gone.

I DON'T KNOW why it threw me in such a tizzy that Aaron was gone. I guess it was because I didn't expect it. He'd never said anything about wanting to move on, and I like to think he would have told me, or that at least I would have picked up some sort of hint that he was looking for a change.

I willed my hands to stop shaking, because there was no way I was going to let on to the tour group that I was having an interior meltdown. I had a job to do, and I took it a lot more seriously than I ever did in my roles in Dad's films.

I promised myself a vodka martini with extra olives after everyone was gone, told them all about Valentino's Lady in Black who leaves roses in the vase by his spot in the tomb, recounted what I knew about what had been filmed here, and swept my group back into the SUV.

During the ride back to the Ballington, in between pointing out other haunted sites and telling stories, I asked my Iowan tourists about what else they'd seen, letting them do the work. A basic trick: make the other person feel special and important.

By the time we arrived, I had most of my equilibrium back. I parked out front, and the sight of my sweet hotel made me feel a little better, as it always did.

Covered with a slightly pinky stucco, the building was fairly standard for turn-of-the-century Southern California. Unusually, though, the entrance was set back from the sidewalk by—

"Oh, what an adorable little courtyard!" one of the adult sisters said.

Exactly what I was going to say. I'd fallen in love with the Ballington right here on the light grey paving stones, shaded by enormous ficuses.

The kid with the Mickey top hat tugged on his shirt and asked for a penny for the fountain.

The low, rectangular fountain had four small dolphins at each corner, spitting into the center, hitting the water around the central, taller, round carved basin that had a mini-fountain at its center. Along with the trees, it helped keep the courtyard relatively cool.

I skirted the fountain and walked up to the heavy glass

double doors, the tour group behind me under the carved stone archway.

I set my hand on the heavy brass knob. I couldn't see inside because of the tinting on the glass, just a vague sense of the mahogany check-in counter on the left and the edge of the burgundy-and-gold carpet.

For a moment, I couldn't turn the knob. My lungs labored; I felt like I was breathing through sludge. My hand, my body, was paralyzed with fear (oh, *that's* what it feels like).

What if I opened the door and found all my friends—Sam, Janie, Marla, Curtis—gone? Vanished without a by-your-leave just like Aaron. Without so much as a "See ya."

I felt (sensed, really) a hand patting my hip.

A hand made of ice cubes.

I looked down. Maggie looked up at me. She nodded, solemn as ever. Still, I thought I understood what she was trying to tell me.

This is what my life had become: I was taking advice and support from a mute six-year-old girl ghost.

Okay. Here went nothing.

I opened the door. "Ladies and gentlemen, welcome to the Ballington, one of Hollywood's most haunted hotels."

FOUR

"IS it okay if we take pictures?" one of the women asked—Sandy, I remembered her name was. The main mom. "We have a Craftsman house back home, and I just love the old architectural details."

I felt a little *squee* of pride. I loved my Ballington, I surely did. *Geek.*

The two-story foyer had pale marble columns, each ringed with a dark brown leather seat; the tops of the columns glinted with gold leaf. The walls were deep red; on the ceiling, dark wood beams gleamed in the chandelier light.

I'd hired someone to go up there and dust the chandeliers. Because, nuh-uh.

"I'm still working on the restoration, so be kind," I said. "And Hollywood Hauntings takes no responsibility for the quality of the photos, as ghosts are known to distort images."

"You really think we're going to sue you if our photos don't come out?" Jeff, Sandy's husband, asked. "That's so Californian."

I flashed him a grin, no offense taken. "Just part of the Hollywood experience—I wouldn't want to disappoint you."

He laughed. I mentally high-fived myself for diffusing the situation.

I caught a flash of movement out of the corner of my eye. I turned my head just a fraction. Sam tilted his hat at me: the signal that everything was ready and in place.

Sam, Janie, Marla, and Curtis hadn't all died in the Ballington, but they'd all had some fond connection with the place over the years. Sam had, in fact, had a standing room here as part of his business—he really *was* a private detective in the 1940s. He's got that Bogart square chin and receding hairline, and while he tries to be all stern and serious, there's nothing better in this world (well, the afterlife, I guess) than his laugh. I do whatever I can to spark it.

"Now," I said to the tour group, "we're still cataloging the spirits we believe haunt the Ballington Hotel. We know there's paranormal activity here; we're just still trying to pinpoint who's doing what. It's not as if the ghosts volunteer that information."

I heard Curtis snicker.

Curtis never made it out of the '80s. Which is too bad, because it looks like they're coming back, between all the hair band reunion tours and the clothes and jewelry that have been showing up in Hot Topic. Curtis had lived here after it had been turned from a hotel into apartments, where apparently he'd had some wild parties. He died in a cocaine-fueled car crash, though; I think it was on Mulholland, or maybe Latigo Canyon.

(Thankfully, even though ghosts are stuck in the clothes they were wearing, they're not stuck with the injuries or wounds or whatever caused their deaths. *That* was a blessing for me, otherwise my life would be a horror movie.)

Right now, I ignored Curtis.

"We've unearthed some reports that during Prohibition, this hotel was used by rum runners to distribute their illegal alcohol. There's also evidence that the basement was used as a speakeasy. We'd eventually like to reopen it as a bar."

"What's a speakeasy?" one of the kids asked.

I looked at the moms for guidance on how much to explain.

"There was a time when alcohol wasn't legal," not-the-Sandy said, bending over to be closer to the children's height. "A speakeasy was a name for an illegal bar during that time."

"Prohibition—that's what they called that time period—was from 1920 to 1933," I added. "This hotel was built in 1923."

Before we left the lobby, I noted the Rennie Macintosh-inspired windows flanking the front door. Then I led them into one of the parlors, with dark red walls above polished beadboard, a carved fireplace that would make Jesus weep, and a settee I'd rescued from an alley and had refinished. The books on the built-in shelves had been carefully sought out through months of lurking in quality used bookshops.

A crystal decanter of whisky and a set of eight matching glasses were arranged on a cherrywood sideboard covered with antique lace. I have to admit it looked tempting, just a sip to soothe my nerves. But Sam was already standing there, a glass in his hand (invisible to everyone but me). When I saw him I sighed in relief, my thighs as weak as Lindsay Lohan's excuses.

He tipped his glass at me, then reached out and gave the sideboard a shake. Glassware shivered and tinkled.

"Was that an earthquake?" Sandy asked. The other mom drew her kid to her side, a hand wrapped around the poor kid's head so he was looking out of only one eye. Instead of struggling, he had a resigned look on his face.

"I don't think so," I said. "The rest of the room isn't shaking."

Sam shoved the sideboard again, the whisky sloshing in the decanter.

"This room was the smoking room, a place for men to retire after supper and discuss...well, things they didn't want to include the women in," I said. "By the forties, the women were protesting that, but old habits die hard. Given the paranormal activity in this room, we believe there must have been a fight—really, you get men together drinking, so it's not a surprise—and someone must have been killed. We do know there was a detective who lived at the hotel at one point. Perhaps he's involved?"

I directed everyone's attention to a portrait of Janie on the wall. A true Bohemian of her day, she was wearing a loose silk caftan, scarlet with a gold Asian pattern picked out, but her slender curves were visible (and, I daresay, a hint of pouting nipple). She lazily balanced one of those long cigarette holders between her forefinger and middle finger.

Tall and slender, she still wears a gold-and-black flapper dress beaded to the nth degree and then some. Because, you see, ghosts have to wear whatever they died in. (This is why your mother tells you to wear clean underwear, just in case.) Her black bobbed hair and bright red lipstick were both a brilliant contrast to her pale skin. She's effing gorgeous, and somehow ethereal (I mean, I think she always was like that, not just since she became a ghost), which puts her looks at total odds with her past: she wasn't just a flapper, she was a bootlegger—and damn good at it, if her stories are true.

I want to grow up and be her, I swear.

For Janie, the Ballington had been the venue where the clandestine rumrunner meetings had taken place, and that, she says, was when she'd truly felt alive and a part of things. The adrenaline rush, the risk-taking, never knowing if you'd be caught. Surviving by your wits. The way she describes it, it sounds like a blast.

"Jane Parker was a queen of the rumrunners in her day," I said. "We believe she's responsible for the speakeasy. Thank goodness for every anti-Prohibitionists' stance, or that detective might never have patronized the establishment twenty years later."

I waved my hand back at the sideboard, and then murmured, surprise in my voice, "Well, would you look at that."

One of the glasses had two fingers of whiskey in it now. Sam winked at me, and it was all I could do not to give him a thumbs-up.

"How did you...?" Jeff asked.

"I didn't do anything," I said truthfully. "I was standing here the whole time. You know men and their drinks, though...maybe the habit survives beyond the grave."

The elevator was next. It was the old-fashioned kind that required me to manually first close the outer brass latticework door. The elevator rocked a little as I did so.

"Don't worry, the mechanics have been fully upgraded," I said when someone squeaked. "It wouldn't be good for business if I trapped tour groups in here on a regular basis, right?"

I used a light tone and mild humor to mask what I was really feeling. Once you've been mobbed by paparazzi, you get a little claustrophobic. Being in an elevator with ten other people, even if two of them were dead, triggered issues for me. I knew the cardinal rule, though: Never let 'em see you sweat.

Or smell you, for that matter. Thank God for heavy-duty deodorant.

Janie didn't become fully visible, but she got to enough corporeality that she could push the button for the tenth floor. Unfortunately, nobody ever noticed that I never chose where the elevator would go, but it amused Janie and me, and if you can't enjoy your work...

This time, the kid who'd seemed to notice Maggie in the van squinted suspiciously at the elevator's control panel. Or maybe it was just gas. It was hard to tell when the lights flickered (thanks, Janie), making the passengers tense just a little bit before we reached our floor.

Atmosphere, baby. Give 'em atmosphere, and they'll follow you anywhere.

Everyone breathed some degree of sighs of relief when we hit our floor and the elevator door opened. The men suppressed theirs well; I did even better.

I led them down the hall, which still had its original, albeit much-worn, Oriental carpeting in faded peacock colors, to Room 113. Of course.

Here was one of the places where I totally made shit up. I mean, it would be an invasion of Marla's privacy to announce her super-secret affair with Jim Morrison. Plus wouldn't it be an invasion of Jim's privacy? Did that depend on whether he'd stuck around as a ghost or moved on to the next plane?

Ugh. Philosophical questions make my skull throb.

"Legend has it that a young woman committed suicide in this room," I said. (Not Marla. Marla had been stoned and turned on a gas stove to make a frozen pizza, and then fallen asleep.)

I glanced at both the kids and the moms, keeping an eye out for negative reactions. Given the presence of children, I'd already decided to abandon the "unwanted pregnancy" portion of the story. Irate parents meant negative publicity for Hollywood Hauntings.

"How did she kill herself?" the oldest girl asked. Cool. Usually it was the boys who were bloodthirsty. Then again, the girl had on a bit too much eyeliner and more black clothing than was comfortable in the southern California summer. She very well could be a Midwestern Wannabe Goth.

Aw. Cute.

"There are conflicting stories," I said. "Some say she hung herself from the closet rod." I opened the closet, braced for the inevitable gasps. I'd hung some nice white dresses in there, a cheap and easy way to startle the tours.

"Others say she jumped out the window."

They all turned to contemplate the casement window where, despite the window being closed, the curtains should have been waving gently in an unfelt breeze.

Nothing was happening.

The unease, the nerves I'd felt before, threatened to burgeon into full-blown anxiety. Where the hell was Marla? Had something happened to her, too?

Go to your happy place, Nikki. I closed my eyes for a moment, conjuring up warm sand and cold ocean water and the perfect wave beneath my board. Deep breath.

Maybe Marla just forgot. It had been known to happen. I couldn't really call out to her, so there was no way to find out.

Rationalize, rationalize. Wouldn't Sam or Janie have

indicated if something was wrong? Of course they would have.

My left thigh was icy cold. I looked down. Maggie was standing *really* close to me. Dammit, I wish she could talk. At least she wasn't waving and mouthing "Bye-bye" again.

"Okay," I said brightly, "we have one more stop before tea. The hotel's not big enough to have a room 666, but we do have a 66..."

Down the elevator. More flickering lights. I tried to flash Janie an "everyone okay?" look, but Goth Girl had decided to pick my brains about spectral activity and EMF meters and stuff like that. I was impressed and welcomed the distraction. She knew more than I'd expected. Turned out she really loved *Ghost Hunters*. Me, too.

So just for grins, I told her I was a Sensitive, so I didn't need equipment.

I don't know if I'm a Sensitive; I'm not sure *what* I am with regards to my ability.

As I understand it, true, full Sensitives are rare, like musical geniuses and child prodigies. Real Sensitives are Wi-Fi'd in to the other plane (or planes? Not clear on that.) —the spirit world, the sixth sense. They can talk to ghosts, mind-read, astral project, the works. If it's paranormal, they can do it.

Me, I can only do the talking-to-ghosts things. The closest I can get to flying out of my body is when I'm surfing.

Solange is a true Sensitive—the only one I've met, in fact. Do you know how many mediums there are in the greater Los Angeles area? And how many of them are fake?

That would be pretty much all of them.

Anyway, I told Goth Girl I wasn't into equipment, that I believed in trusting your instincts. Seeing or feeling or hearing something made more sense to me than having faith in some machine that goes *ping*.

"But what about special effects? Holograms? Funky wiring?" she asked.

"Are you suggesting I do that here?" I asked, raising an eyebrow. I'd perfected that for a role when I was her age.

Her kohl-rimmed eyes widened, and she had the grace to look abashed. Go her.

"No...but it *is* Hollywood."

"Well, if I could afford a special effects guy, I'd probably hire a team to make this tour more whizzbang," I said as I led everyone down the hall. "But it all comes back to trusting your gut. If you're really tuned in, you'll know whether something's fake or not."

In Room 66, Curtis didn't let me down. He slammed the door behind us; the two littlest kids jumped, but didn't have meltdowns, for which I was truly grateful. He also made some jazz fade in and out. He didn't much like jazz, but I'd managed to convince him that A Flock of Seagulls just wasn't spooky—unless you were talking about their hair. (What *had* they been thinking?)

I spun the tale of a police raid on the bootleggers, gunshots ("See that hole there?") as Curtis slowly lowered the temperature—for one person at a time. The kid who might or might not have seen Maggie and Janie stiffened, staring. The other little kid wrapped himself around his mother's leg.

I fudged these stories, of course, out of deference to my friends. I also never asked them to be involved in the room/tale that was closest to their lives; Sam hadn't died in the parlor, and Janie had no connection to the elevator, and Curtis had nothing to do with Room 66.

I tried to open the door, pretended it was stuck, and asked Jeff to try.

He tugged, rattling the knob, as Curtis kept his own hand clamped down on it. "Damn, it's so cold!" Jeff said, just as Curtis let go and the door flew open.

I shrieked, because there was someone standing outside.

FIVE

"WHAT? WHAT IS IT?" several voices said.

"Didn't you see that?" I asked, falling back into my role even as I willed air into my lungs again. I hadn't expected anyone—no, honest, this wasn't part of the tour—and I was on just enough of an edge that the sight of Marla standing there, hands over mouth and eyes wide because she'd realized she'd completely missed her cue, had completely freaked me out.

They might be my friends, but they could still scare the living shit out of me.

"See what?" Goth Girl, Spooky Kid, and Jeff all asked.

I smiled mysteriously. "Why, another ghost, of course. That concludes the official tour of the Ballington Hotel—now we'll have some refreshments in the dining room and see if anything else crops up."

The dining room, for all its dark wood paneling and blue-and-gold carpet and heavy tables, was surprisingly light, because the upper half of one wall was a bank of windows looking into the solarium. The white tablecloths helped as well.

On a sideboard, the tea sandwiches and tarts were laid out, with the clotted cream and jam and lemon curd in pretty little crystal dishes with cute little silver spoons. The pots of tea steamed on a cart, where Solange would serve from. The AC was nudged up just a skosh to balance out the hot tea.

The dining room smelled sweetly of flowers; Solange had tucked fresh ones into low ceramic vases for the two tables near the solarium windows, where I indicated the group be seated.

Solange was waiting by the tea cart. She wore a long, flowing, multicolored skirt, floaty scarves, and chunky jewelry embedded with crystals and hematite. A bit OTT, but the tourists liked it.

"Everyone, this is Solange. She's going to help get you settled with your tea, and then, if anyone wants, she'll tell your fortune—and if there's anyone you'd like to contact, she's here to give it a try."

There were some oohs and aahs, although Goth Girl rolled her eyes. No surprise there. Honestly, if anyone thought this part of the tour wasn't staged, they deserved the fortune they got, although Solange was spooky-good at what she did.

I'd met Solange when I walked into Star Dust—a New Age shop in Venice Beach, where she worked part-time as a clerk and medium—after I'd gotten out of rehab-cum-spa and was looking for information about ghosts. We became fast friends, not just because she believed that I could see ghosts. For the tours, she prepped the food, helped serve it, and did Tarot readings and telling stories about spirits and other spooky stuff.

I left them all in the dining room near the windows that overlooked the solarium, and headed for the kitchen.

There was an assortment of little sandwiches—one of each, except two of cheddar and Branston pickle—and that lime curd tart, left by Solange. How had she known?

The electric kettle was just about to boil.

"Thanks, Janie," I said aloud, even though I couldn't see her. Yes, Janie knew when I needed tea, and could manifest enough to plug in the kettle, bless her heart.

My stomach was still jumpy as I poured water over the metal tea strainer into the cup. I inhaled the familiar scent of bergamot, trying to calm myself. My grandmother had loved Earl Grey.

I wished Grandma Rosa were here so I could ask her a few damn questions.

And give her a hug again, even if it would feel all cold and squicky. It would still be a hug with Grandma.

Why hadn't she loved me enough to stay with me after death?

BACK IN THE DINING ROOM, I listened to Solange do her spiel and answered more questions about ghosts, historic Hollywood, and the like. A few minutes before it was time to take the group back to their hotel, Solange and I slipped into the foyer for a quick recap.

"Don't you worry about anything here," she said. "I know you've got a full schedule this evening. I'll clean up, and lock up when I leave."

I hugged her, which always took a little maneuvering because she was taller than me (many people are) and that put her boobs in a potentially awkward place. "Thank you," I said. "I didn't think you'd remember about the premiere."

"*Cher*, you've been obsessing about it for weeks."

Oh. She was probably right. I hadn't been out in public like this since I'd gotten out of rehab, and as proud as I was for my father (the reason I was going), I was still unusually nervous. Plus, of course, the potential for the usual family drama.

"Oh," she added, "and before I forget—" She reached into her pocket and produced a bag of midnight-blue muslin tied with a silver cord, the whole thing small enough to fit in my palm. When she handed it to me, I caught the scent of herbs. I'm crap at identifying them, but suffice to say they didn't smell like something that would get me arrested for possession.

"Mulberry and pennyroyal for protection and strength, and a crystal blessed with rosemary oil," Solange said. "I knew I had to keep it small so it'll fit in one of those tiny-ass excuses for a purse you'll be carrying."

"Wow," I said, staring down at it. I actually felt a little annoying lump in my throat, touched at her thoughtfulness, that she'd planned ahead to make this for me. "Um, thank you."

She laughed that hearty laugh of hers and hugged me again. "Okay, *cher*—get back in there before the guests start throwing the china. You have things to do."

AFTER I DROPPED the Midwest contingent off at their hotel, I swung by the historic Roosevelt Hotel on Hollywood Boulevard. It was three o'clock, hot and blinding. I really wanted to talk to Solange, but I had family obligations tonight. Yippie. But even though I was cutting it close, time-wise, I had another source I could consult.

The Roosevelt was dim, quiet in contrast to the bustling

touristy street outside. Its two-story lobby boasted 1920s Spanish Colonial columns and a beamed ceiling painted with heraldic symbols, and somehow it always has a church-like feel. Music and quiet words floated from the Cinegrill bar, but it wasn't a prime time for drinkers—or anyone else, for that matter. Not quite happy hour yet.

Which meant the ladies' room was empty when I entered. I checked beneath the dark, hammered-wood stall doors just to be safe. The copper sinks gleamed beneath the amber light sconces, and the place smelled of lemony fresh cleaner. Classy.

"Marilyn?" I asked, my voice echoing in the cavernous room.

She appeared in the mirror second from the door. Generally she was known for appearing in the mirror in the hallway off the lobby, but I happened to know she preferred to hang out in here.

I don't know her real name, so I call her Marilyn. She's extremely cool with that.

So there she was in the mirror, all poofy blond hair and pouty lips and heavy-lidded eyes and swirling white dress. Her eyes widened when she recognized me.

"Nikki! It's been forever!"

"Pretty close to," I said, although it hadn't been more than a few months. The Roosevelt wasn't a popular nightspot for the young crowd—not that I got invited to parties anymore. But I did like to keep in touch with Marilyn. As much as she loved her "job," she got lonely sometimes.

I sat with my hip up on the counter. "You heard anything weird on the streets?"

She cocked her pretty head. "Like what?"

"Aaron Schwabach at Hollywood Forever is gone."

She reared back. "Gone? Gone how?"

"Gone gone. I don't know how. He's just not there anymore."

"How can that be?"

I resisted rolling my eyes. "Your guess is as good as mine."

"Oh dear." She paced in the mirror, disappearing and reappearing, hand to her lips. "I don't know him well; I never go there, he never comes here. But I hadn't heard he was planning to move on."

"Is there anyone else who might have heard about it?"

She shook her head. "I'm usually up on the gossip."

"What might encourage him to do something like this?"

Her shrug was graceful, practiced. "Tired. Bored. Maybe someone he loved recently passed, so he had someone to meet on the other side."

Hm. I hadn't thought of that. A child, maybe? I assumed he was old enough when he died, plus the years since he'd died, that someone of his own generation would be long gone. I had no idea if Aaron had had children, though. I'd have to look in to that.

I glanced at my iPhone for the time. Crap. Research would have to wait.

"You'll let me know if you hear anything through the lines?" I asked.

"Of course, dear." Marilyn-in-the-mirror touched my reflection's cheek, and I felt it on this side. Spoooooky.

I blew her a kiss and headed back out.

I was late, late, for a very important date.

Okay, not a very important one for me, but for other people, it was akin to life or death.

SIX

AND SINCE I never wanted to disappoint my mother (which is not to say I didn't do so on a regular basis—to say she was easily peeved with me would be an understatement), I double-timed it into Brentwood, punched in my security code, then rolled up the curving driveway to the Ashburne family estate.

A.k.a. my home.

Well, I live at the Ballington. I'd had a suite of rooms fixed up there, and my attorney had had my mail forwarded there and everything. But it was hard to say that the mansion I'd grown up in wasn't my home, and because my parents couldn't conceive of me *not* living there, I still had a bunch of stuff in my old rooms.

And a bunch of memories in the guest house where my grandmother had lived, but we won't talk about that now.

Sloping, impeccably green lawns on either side. A delightful succulent garden with a bright mosaic fountain in the center. And then the house, a white stucco monstrosity spreading out in both directions like a benevolent shepherd welcoming you into the arms of his flock.

Talk about unsettling. Thankfully my parents weren't hyper-religious, or this whole experience would have been even more painful.

I'd switched cars; I was in my beloved, if several years old, British racing green Mini. I parked it carefully in front of the house, leaving the keys inside and grabbing my overnight bags. The car would be taken care of. Washed and waxed, the engine checked.

Yeah, hi, and welcome to my life of insane excess. It wouldn't help for me to protest. The car would still be taken care of.

It's an amazing way to grow up. I won't say it didn't have its perks, that I didn't—don't—appreciate the benefits, the opportunities.

But when your house is made fun of on a regular basis, it kind of skews everything in your head. It's one thing to have a lavish Hollywood mansion; it's another to have your own planetarium. At least we didn't have a present-wrapping room. (Oops. Was that my outside voice?)

I let myself in, dropped my bags in the two-story vaulted monstrosity of a foyer (they'd be taken upstairs and unpacked), and wandered in the direction of the sun room, a glassed-in gazebo that my father used as a study.

His desk was glass-topped, keeping with the airy open feel of the room, which looked out on a garden of grapevine arbors and topiaries and a fountain, like a Tuscan villa exterior. Awards he'd won were displayed on minimalist floating shelves, and white boards on easels were covered with his scribbled notes on current and upcoming projects.

Even in crisp jeans and a button-down blue-striped shirt, he looked impeccable. He wasn't wearing a tie, and he rarely did, much to my mother's dismay. At his level, if anyone cared about his lack of tie, they kept their mouth firmly shut. His hair was greying; I happened to know he had it selectively dyed—just enough to keep him looking distinguished but not tipping over into the "old" description.

"Nikki!" My father, the illustrious Edward Ashburne, set down the latest issue of *Variety* and stood to hug me.

"Hi, Daddy." I stood on tiptoe and kissed him on the cheek. He's average height, but next to me, he's tall. My baby-brother-by-three-years Ned takes after him. I wondered if Ned had arrived yet.

As if reading my mind, my father said, "You'd better go upstairs. Your mother is frantic because both you and Ned are late."

"I'm exactly on time," I protested.

"You're a few minutes early," he said. "But not in your mother's world. Ned called; he's on his way."

"Let me guess: he's just turning off San Vicente?" No matter where he was, he always said he was just turning off San Vicente, almost home.

Daddy tapped me on the nose, a gesture that took me back to my childhood. "Well spotted."

Ned would arrive, smelling of brine, his hair a mess, grinning like the village idiot. I was jealous. Plus Ned didn't even have to get fitted for anything; he had several tuxes in his room-sized closet.

Which reminded me to make the ascent into the night-mare above. And I bet you thought hell was below.

I was also sad, because surfing used to be the thing Ned and I did together. But ever since I told him I could see ghosts and he decided I was lying, he had barely spoken to me. I was persona non grata.

Persona non ghosta.

I missed him. A lot.

I swung by the vast kitchen to snag a bottle of flavored water, then ascended the sweeping double staircase to the second floor. My mother's suite was down the hall; the double doors to her sitting room were open.

My mother was pinned down by the manicurist and the stylist when I arrived in her sitting room. I didn't even have time to do the air-kissing thing with her—we'd never shared outrageous displays of affection—because Susie, who'd been hovering nearby, shooed me towards the dressing room.

My mother was always a little aloof, despite the fact that I knew, somewhere, deep down, that she loved me. She'd resented me a little ever since I turned twenty, because she could no longer claim to be thirty-nine (unless she wanted to admit to a teenage pregnancy, which was at least as bad as being over forty).

I'm not even sure *I* know my mother's real age. Discreet but regular plastic surgery helped fool everyone. Well, to a certain extent. You'd never mistake her for twenty-five.

Her hair was expensively blond and in the process of being expertly coiffed for the event this evening, so she smelled of hairspray and Chanel. She wore a red satin robe in preparation for changing into her fancy dress in time to leave.

"Nikki!" my mother said. "Go with Susie to try on your outfit."

"Hello, Mom," I said. "I love you, too."

I followed Susie into my mother's massive closet. It was bigger than some apartments I'd been in. As a child, I'd loved the multiple mirrors, lost in the fantasy of multiple me's and the sense of infinity. Now...now I always expected to see someone dead looking over my shoulder.

Kinda kills the desire to check yourself out in storefront windows, you know?

My dress for the premiere fit me perfectly. Custom tailoring FTW.

It was grey, but a shimmery steel grey that still commanded some attention. It had more of a scoop neckline, which was more than enough for me and necessitating a halter bra, which wasn't easy to find in my size, so more custom work had been done. The dress had a funky little mermaid-tail flounce at the back of the skirt, and the figure-hugging bias cut of the dress really looked sweet on me.

I shimmied back out of the dress, grabbed an extra robe—something light and turquoise and smelling of Chanel—and steeled myself to reenter the bedroom.

It wasn't that I didn't like to be pampered. I mean, who doesn't like that? Spa days are my friends. It was more that I didn't like to argue, and I had a strong suspicion the stylist and I were going to have words.

Within moments I was ensconced in a chair getting a mani and pedi, a pale pink polish to compliment the dress. The manicurist wanted to do tips, but I refused. With all the work I do on the hotel, they'd just go to waste.

Charee—who used to be Charles, go her—our usual stylist, fluffed her hands through my hair. "Oh honey," she said, "your hair is always like silk. And so thick. We never have to do a weave. But the style... Short and curly just isn't in."

"I like it this way," I said. I mean, it's not like I don't take care of it.

I can't really explain why I'm so obsessed with not changing my hair. I used to wear it long and straight, which I know was like everyone else, but it did look good on me, too, making my face look thinner. There was a lot I could play with, too, like twisting it up so it sprayed out the back of my head, or adding colored strands.

"Please let me put in extensions," she said. "Just down to here—" she indicated my scapula "—and then—"

"No," I said.

I didn't cut my hair right after Grandma Rosa, nor after the OD. I did it when I bought the hotel. Long got in the way when I was scraping wallpaper and regrouting original tile, even if it was pulled back.

Then, slowly, I realized the new haircut represented the new me. The old hair was Nikki, vapid party girl. The new hair was...Nikki. Whoever Nikki was now.

Charee sighed the heavy sigh of someone being deeply oppressed. "Can I just straighten it? It'll still be the cute bob, but..."

"No, thanks," I said. It was a tiny bit tempting, but I just didn't want to.

Shades of the old me, just running off and doing what I wanted and pouting when I was thwarted.

The new me and the old me, they were gonna have words in the back alley later.

"I'm sorry, Charee, but I'm happy with this," I added. "Can you work with what you've got? Fluff it up a little, maybe add some sparkly clips to go with dress?"

Her eyes lit up at the concept of sparkly clips, and I was glad I'd found a compromise that didn't involve a standoff with curling irons at dawn.

When I was fluffed and buffed and processed and dressed, I checked myself out in the hall of mirrors, and I was pretty happy with what I saw. I'd let the makeup guy have fun, and he'd matched my eye shadow to my nail polish. It was a little sci-fi-ish, but I kinda liked it; it really made my eyes stand out.

I think Maggie liked it, too. She looked up at me and giggled silently, her hand over her mouth.

I giggled back at her. Better to be giddy than having the world's biggest breakdown about my first official public appearance in almost a year.

Because oh yeah, I'd been deliberately avoiding thinking about it until now.

On one hand, it was silly. I'd been in the public eye since I was a child, when I'd done some modeling and TV commercials. Hell, I used to get paid ridiculous amounts of money to dress up and sparkle and smile and party, to be a guest at a nightclub opening or whatever.

But that had been the old Nikki, the one with the long, straight hair because long, straight hair was in, the one who didn't have a care in the world, the one who was popular and loved.

No idea who that girl was. I barely remember her sometimes.

My family had enough clout to shield me from the worst of the prying questions and reporters after my rehab stint, Donny the paparazzo notwithstanding. But that didn't mean a few hadn't slipped through, finding my personal e-mail or spotting me somewhere, descending like a plague of locusts wanting a quote.

I'd chosen a different life, one out of the public eye for the most part.

But I'm human. I still cared whether people liked me.

What if nobody liked me anymore? My former friends had mostly abandoned me, and my brother was mad enough at me to basically not be speaking to me.

I didn't need public adulation but...but...but what if nobody cared about me anymore?

Choosing to be private and having nobody care about you were two very different things.

And then there was the problem of the star of *Day Into*

Knight, whom of course I'd see tonight: Evan Frohman. That's right, my pre-near-death crush.

Gah. It was enough to make a girl run home to her ghost friends.

But I'd made a promise to my father. I squared my shoulders. I had a job to do.

SEVEN

MOM and I met up with Dad and Ned downstairs in the sun room/study. Even I had to admit my dad looked pretty rockin' in his tux. He looked as if he could take on the world, but totally approachable at the same time. Or maybe that's just me.

He hugged me gently so he didn't muss me. I turned to Ned, but before either of us could say anything, Susie appeared with her ever-present organizer and pile of paperwork to shoo us out the door. It would never do for the producer to be late to his own movie premiere.

Then it was into the limo and off to the El Capitan Theatre on Hollywood Boulevard.

Day into Knight was about a group of typical college frat boys who immerse themselves in a camp that teaches them what it took to be a medieval knight. Not just jousting and sword fighting, but dancing and chess and the concepts of chivalry and honor and courtly love. Will they be able to use their new hawt skillz to charm the ladies and win the girls of their dreams?

Of course they will. Remember, this is one of Edward Ashburne's kinder, gentler movies.

A few years ago, my father decided that his reputation as the king of the teen sex comedy needed to change. The times were changing, he said, and he needed to roll with that. His uncanny ability to predict the future worked for him again, because his foray into family fare was even more lucrative—and that was saying a lot.

Somehow, he'd managed to find a balance between romantic and witty for the adults with fun for the kids.

As such, he wanted the whole family at this premiere to show off his "image."

Savvy man, my dad.

I'd known this day was coming for a while, but I'd kind of tried to pretend it didn't exist in my reality. In a way, it didn't—I'm not sure the Hollywood premiere scene *is* my reality anymore.

But sliding into the limo, knowing I looked fantastic because I'd been fawned over by professionals, I felt a little squee of excitement in my belly. The lights, the attention… there was a lot to like about that.

Daddy popped open the champagne and poured some for all of us. Ahh, there's nothing like good champagne. Darling little bubbles of delight, oh, how I adore thee.

So just stop bouncing around in my stomach like you've entered the world of nervous Irish dancing championship, okay?

I wanted to be distracted by catching up with my family, but Ned had his head down and was texting someone. I couldn't see who because he was sitting diagonally from me, and I couldn't ask him because of the persona non ghosta thing. My parents were talking about Robertson Waverly's big 50th birthday bash in a couple of days. Well, my mother was talking and my father was smiling indulgently. It was my mother's chosen job to make my father look even more spectacular than he already is, and she took that job very seriously.

I'd talk to Maggie, but that would've weirded everyone out. Plus the whole one-sided conversation thing. I'd already explained to her that I wanted my picture taken tonight, so she wouldn't be able to be at my side. She could wait in the limo, or she could go into the theatre and meet me there if she wanted to see the movie.

Here's something I don't know: if you die at a certain age and become a ghost, how much do you get to mature mentally and emotionally? Since Maggie won't talk to me, I really can't tell.

Questions like that make my head hurt, so I avoid them, normally.

We pulled up outside the theatre, and my nerves went all aflutter again, but then I stepped out of the limo, accepting the proffered hand of help from the driver. The strobe-like flashes transported me back.

Deep breath. Showtime.

I tossed my hair with practiced ease and slipped into the "slimming pose," slightly turned, one leg partially in front of the other. I smiled, stretched my neck just enough so that the lights wouldn't cast shadows under my chin.

The red carpet was short—this wasn't an awards show—and so we stopped almost immediately for a quick interview. I stood next to my father, giving him an adoring gaze to show my support.

Lots of near-blinding flashes as photogs took shots of the happy, supportive family.

Call me naïve, but I really didn't expect the first question to be thrown my way.

"Nikki, how does it feel to be back in the limelight?"

I...uh...*what*? You talkin' to me?

I scrambled to recover. "I'm not in the limelight," I said. "Tonight's my father's night to shine. *Day Into Knight* is a fantastic movie."

"But what have you been doing with yourself for the past year?"

From the crowd, someone shouted, "Rehab?"

Ah, shit.

Keeping the smile firmly plastered on my face, I said, "I'd be happy to answer questions about *Day Into Knight*, but really, you should be talking to my father. If you'll excuse me."

I made a show of standing on tiptoe to kiss my father on the cheek—cameras flashed like fireworks—and then I waved to the crowd as I went towards the theatre entrance.

Okay, I kinda sashayed. The cut of the dress just begged for it. And I don't do a gazillion lunges with my trainer to not show off my butt just a little, you know?

Evan Frohman and Jesse D'Esposito were just ahead of our party, which I hadn't noticed until I got closer to the theatre doors. They were giving their last waves before going in.

They looked back and saw me, so I smiled. Although I'd never met Jesse, I knew Evan would recognize me.

Their eyes did that shifty "Oh, I wasn't really looking at you, sorry, thought you were someone else" thing, and they looked right through me, and then they went inside.

Really? Seriously?

I went inside, too, but they'd already retreated to the other end of the lobby. I swear I saw Jesse shake his head and mouth something that might have been "trouble"—or maybe it was "crazy"—while Even pretended not to look at me, even though he was.

I repeat, really? When did I become the one to shun to avoid looking bad? I mean, okay, sure, I'd been laying low, but did that mean I was bad for your precious reputation?

My family caught up with me at that point, and I did my best to shake the cloud off. To do that Zen thing my therapist was always trying to teach me about.

Let it go. It doesn't matter what they think.

Of course it mattered. Don't kid about that. I just wasn't going to let it bother me right now, so help me, if it was the last thing I did.

There were more interviews inside, by more reputable media who actually wanted to focus on the movie. One did ask why I didn't have a part in *Day Into Knight*, which was a valid enough question.

My father put his arm around me and said, "Nikki's pursuing other interests right now."

The interviewer swung towards me. "Oh?"

"Historic restoration and early twentieth-century architecture," I said.

There. That didn't sound like a euphemism for rehab, now did it? It made me sound erudite.

Or pathetic. There's a fine line, you know. I suspected I was firmly on the wrong side of it.

I COULDN'T FOCUS on the movie; my thoughts kept drifting back to Evan and Jesse's clear dis, which left a heavy block of ice in my gut that wouldn't melt. My dad had started working on *Day Into Knight* before I OD'd, and had asked my thoughts on a few ideas and plot points. I'd suggested rewordings of a few lines in the script, and everyone in the audience laughed at those, but even that didn't make me feel better.

In fact—and I'd forgotten this until right this moment— I'm pretty sure I recommended Evan for the part.

Some chivalrous bastard he'd turned out to be.

I shifted, unable to get comfortable in the overly padded seat. Despite the icy knot in my stomach, the theatre felt overly warm, pressing in, while the movie seemed louder than it ought to be, especially the clangy bangy jousting scenes.

Maybe I was just stupid. None of my friends returned my calls anymore; why did I think showing up and smiling would make everyone change their minds? Everything I knew about friendship, I'd learned from the movies: that there were friends-for-life, people who might get annoyed at you or argue with you, but in the end you made up and stayed BFFs forever. You stayed together through thick and thin.

Had I just picked fickle friends? Or was it all a load of bullshit?

My grandmother had talked about Hollywood being a crazy, shallow place, but she hadn't grown up in it like I had. It was normal to me.

I didn't like this "normal" anymore.

Thank God for Solange. Now there was someone who knew my deepest secret and hadn't run away screaming.

And, of course, my ghost friends.

I wanted to be home in my beloved Ballington, hanging out with them, as annoying as some of them could be.

For a few minutes, I'd been able to forget about Aaron being missing. Now that problem started gnawing at me again, too.

As discreetly as I could, I looked up at the opera boxes on either sides of the theatre. I didn't see the resident El Capitan ghosts, but there were actual people sitting in the boxes, so they might have been being discreet themselves.

When I was little, I loved going to the movies—I thought they were magic, even though my father worked on them (okay, I probably thought he was a little magical, too). The fact that I couldn't relax and enjoy this one was seriously starting to piss me off.

I couldn't even enjoy the original, colorful East Indian plaster designs that ringed the theatre.

There was a reception afterwards, and I sipped a glass of champagne and did my dutiful daughter routine for as long as I could stand it. Then I excused myself to find the bathroom, but headed upstairs to the opera boxes instead.

Since the general public had left and only the invited guests remained, there was nobody up here. I would've liked to linger and look at the photos lining the walls—they'd turned the balcony promenade into a Wall of Fame—but I didn't want to be gone for long, lest my mother notice and frown. (Just kidding. Botox doesn't allow that.)

Some might call the story of the El Capitan ghosts a *Romeo and Juliet* love story, which is ridiculous because *Romeo and Juliet* is a freaking *tragedy*—plus neither of the ghosts here committed suicide for love, because that ain't love.

Anyway. Thomas worked here in the late 1920s when the theatre was an actual stage theatre. He says he was talented, and I'm inclined to believe him, because he's not the boastful type otherwise. He fell in love with the daughter of a frequent patron.

Bertha (hey, it was something like the twentieth most common baby name in the 1920s. Who are we to judge?)

returned the sentiment, despite the status difference. She was considered frail, and he was the first person who didn't mollycoddle her. They flirted, and fell for each other, hard.

The day they were supposed to run away together, Thomas was killed in a construction accident. Bertha didn't find out until she arrived at the theatre that evening, at which point her unhealthy heart up and gave out.

Thankfully Thomas had waited around for a bit. And since they both loved the theatre—and, later, movies—they'd stayed. Free entry to all the premieres; not too shabby.

They generally watched from the left opera box. The curtain in the hallway hung closed.

"Thomas?" I said. "Bertha? You guys around? It's Nikki."

No response. I repeated my query a little louder as I pushed aside the heavy scarlet velvet.

Nope. Nada.

I went back through the promenade, still calling their names, and around to the other side.

I shoved aside the curtain to the right-side opera box. The box lights were off and the theatre lights were dimmed, so it took my eyes a moment to adjust. I saw movement, assumed it was my friends, and took a step towards—

Oh. Ew...

I wished my eyes hadn't adjusted.

It was Evan, and he was with Chris, my former BFF, and I'm no prude, not by a long shot, but that was an eyeful I never, ever needed to see.

"Jesus, Nikki," Chris said, not even bothering to cover herself. "What is your problem?"

"There's no Bertha here," Evan said. "And you're not invited to make this a threesome."

So much for that family-friendly chivalry Evan's character had learned.

Sadly, I had no witty, cutting comeback. I didn't have a comeback of any kind.

"Weirdo," I heard Chris say.

Cheeks burning, I let the curtain drop.

I checked the bathrooms before going back down to the reception. I didn't have access to many parts of the theatre (including the lower level where they film live talk shows), but I'd never known Thomas or Bertha to hang out down there.

I suppose they could've been hiding away, but they had no reason to. The ice block in my stomach made me feel sick. I was pretty sure—no, I *knew*—that they were gone, too.

I SLEPT at home that night, as did Ned. We both knew better than to argue with our mother over that.

Neither of us live that far away, but Mom wanted to feel like we were having a family thing.

My iPhone scared me into wakefulness with Foreigner's "Urgent." Heart pounding, I had to figure out where I was (those were my framed horse jumping blue ribbons on the wall, so I was at the mansion) and what time it was (barely an hour after I'd fallen asleep). I fumbled for the phone.

Curtis.

Something was very wrong.

Of all the Ballington residents, only Curtis was willing to use the telephone. Although they'd all used phones before they died, the rest of them still shunned the technology. Curtis had always embraced technology. If he were still alive, he'd be giving Bill Gates a run for his money. It's all I can do to keep his grubby ghostly mitts off my iPhone.

Yes, any one of them could have filtered through the innerspace (or whatever) and just popped in to tell me what was going on. But I have a wee problem with people (even dead ones) just showing up in my bedroom in the middle of the night and scaring the pants off of me, so I'd dissuaded them from doing that.

Unfortunately, Curtis's energy (or whatever) generally fries the electronics on their end, so I buy cheap phones for the hotel and replace them frequently.

From the static coming through the line, I knew a replacement was imminent.

"What is it?" I asked.

"It's Curtis," he said, and I refrained from pointing out *again* that I knew that. "Someone's in the hotel."

"Who? What?"

But any details he might have given me were lost in static that crackled so loud, I had to hold the phone away from my ear

"Tell everyone to sit tight until I get there. Do not engage—repeat, do not engage."

I hoped he'd heard me.

I threw on my clothes, grabbed what I needed, left a note in the kitchen (Susie would find it when she got my mother's morning coffee), and was on the road in fifteen minutes.

EIGHT

CURTIS'S CALL shocked me into soberness, but I still kept an eye on my speed as I headed through LA. Even at this time of night, there were cars on the freeways and streets (if there were no cars, it would be a sure sign of an alien invasion or the Rapture), and there would be cops as well, eager to pick off any imbibers stupid enough to get behind the wheel. All told, I hadn't had that much over dinner and when chatting with my dad, and it had been a couple hours ago.

Still, no reason to take chances.

"Why are you speeding?"

"Well, officer, I got a call that someone's broken into my hotel. No, no, there are no guests. One of the ghosts called, you see."

I think not.

Once upon a time I might have been able to pull the "But I'm Nikki Ashburne" card, but that ship had sailed with Paris and Lindsay and Amanda, not to mention the Biebster and my old friend Missy.

Waiting at the stoplight at Venice Boulevard, I tapped

my fingernails on the steering wheel, a bad habit I'd never been able to break. (This was why I didn't normally get manicures anymore—well, this and the whole hotel renovation thing.) Curtis had sounded pretty tense. Before I'd bought the hotel and had all the locks changed, there had been a few homeless folks, but this sounded different.

Still, I couldn't fathom calling 911 just yet.

I cursed myself for lagging on installing an alarm system. To get the entire place wired for an alarm system was a major project—and a major expense—especially when the hotel hadn't been fully upgraded from knob-and-tube electrical wiring. It was on the list, I swear.

Wiring is so not sexy.

Then again, neither is stripping wallpaper.

I eased my Mini by the front of the hotel. Lights were off except for the entrance lights at the front. There were several vehicles I didn't recognize, but that didn't mean a lot. The Ballington was on Wilshire, with public parking for any of the apartment buildings or businesses nearby. There was a private, gated lot in the back for Ballington guests (when it had guests), and space down the alley for service vehicles.

Still, I grabbed my phone and took pictures of the vehicles directly in front, including license plates, just in case.

Sheez. Where was Donny and his pro camera setup when he would have actually been useful?

My sweep of the block done, I pulled into the alley, cutting the lights as I did. I didn't want to waste time checking all the entrances to figure out where the thief (or thieves) had gotten in. I wish I'd thought to ask Curtis, though, in case he knew.

The kitchen door was properly locked. I slipped inside, turning on the small electric-blue Maglite attached to my keychain. In an encounter, I could use it as a weapon; I'd taken a cool self-defense course about that.

Unless there was more than one person, or he/she/they had guns.

Nope. Wasn't gonna think about that.

I listened. From here, everything was quiet.

"Curtis?" I whispered. Then, a little louder, "Curtis! Anyone?"

Damn damn damn. What if something had happened to all of them, just like Aaron and Thomas and Bertha? What if they were *gone*?

I glanced down at Maggie. She wasn't looking at me. She was staring at the swinging double doors that led to the dining room. I couldn't entirely see the look on her face, but I got the sense that she was listening hard.

Or maybe "listening" wasn't the right verb. Sensing? Trying to sense?

Curtis appeared then, right next to me, and I bit back on my yelp and swallowed hard to muffle it. Jaysus, I'll never get used to that. This is why I have the no-bedroom rule. With my nerves so on edge, I'd almost swung out with my flashlight—not that it would have made any difference if I was up against a ghost.

A new thought struck me: What if the *intruder* was a ghost? Curtis hadn't given details on the phone before it went all staticky.

Now, as I opened my mouth to demand details, Marla filtered through the double doors. Which particularly eerie because the doors each have a little round window in them, and I hadn't seen her in the windows.

She looked more wide-eyed and paranoid than usual, which was saying something. And that made me even more nervous about who—or what—I was going up against.

"Where are Sam and Janie?" I kept my voice pitched low, assuming they'd cut me off if anyone else came near. "Are they okay?"

Curtis nodded. "They're watching the guy. That way one of them can report while the other one keeps watch."

I was betting that was Sam's smart arrangement. "Just one guy?" That was good. Better than a slew, anyway.

Both Curtis and Marla nodded.

"Real or ghost?"

"Real," Marla stage-whispered. "But he has stuff with him."

"A gun?" Maybe this wasn't looking up after all.

"No," Curtis said. "Equipment. I think an EMF thingie, that sort of thing. It looks like *Ghostbusters* gear, anyway, but more...modern. Smaller. Sophisticated."

My fear drained away, replaced by pure, clean anger.

"Sonovabitch," I said. "That little weasel." I swung to face Curtis. "Where is he now?"

Curtis blinked out. Marla made a little whimpering noise; I think she felt safer, somehow, when he was here, like she wasn't the only ghost. Maggie didn't count, being a kid, I guess.

I don't spend too much time trying to figure out Marla's tenuous version of "logic." That way led to madness, or at least a headache.

Curtis blinked back a few moments later. At least I was mostly prepared for it this time. "He's in the smoking room."

Of course he was. Would I sound paranoid if I wondered whether someone in one of my tour groups had told him that weird shit happened in the smoking room? Had Sandy or Goth Girl been a spy?

Okay. I *did* sound paranoid. A good benchmark to compare any other crazy thoughts to. Must remember that.

But now, to action. I wanted Curtis with me, but I suspected Marla was about to have a nervous breakdown. I reached out, made the motion of caressing her hair even though I didn't quite touch her. "If you want to go hide somewhere, sweetie, to feel safer, you go right ahead."

She nodded, looking like a frightened, trembling rabbit, and winked out of sight.

I looked down. "Maggie, same goes for you."

She pursed her lips as if considering, then shook her head, curls bouncing.

"Curtis, go on ahead and let me know if he heads this way. I want the element of surprise."

I'd been living in this hotel for a while, and I knew it pretty well—I'd had to deal with a few nights without power, even—so I was able to maneuver through the dining room without bashing into any chairs or tables.

The cavernous foyer was ringed with tall, skinny windows, and the streetlights outside provided ample light, not that I couldn't have made my way between the group-ings of chairs and (impressively fake) potted plants without it. I kept to the inner wall, though, rather than storming directly through the center, even though part of me wanted to.

Wanted to run through screaming with an upraised sword like the doomed hero in a samurai movie. Not that I had a sword, nor much of an idea what to do with one. My self-defense class never covered swords, samurai or other.

I was angry. My space had been violated, and I wanted revenge.

The minute Curtis had said the intruder had ghost-hunting equipment, I'd known exactly who it was. That annoying guy, Rudy, of Ominous Spiritus. The twit who'd e-mailed me, what, five? six? times trying to get a free "personal tour" of the Ballington with all of his equipment.

I'd suspected he was some fly-by-night operation, just him and maybe another fellow geek or two. I couldn't find anything about Ominous Spiritus except for a website that discussed the fact and fallacy of ghosts and spirits and hauntings. Although most of it had been pretty basic, and pretty accurate, the site didn't exactly scream "professional ghost hunters."

More like it squealed "I still live in my mom's basement."

Part of me was sorely tempted to have my ghost posse (sans Marla, of course) go in there, blow his EMF meter to smithereens, and scare the living shit out of him. My strong suspicion was that he'd never encountered any real spirit other than a bounce or two on his equipment, and if he did, he'd probably faint dead away or run screaming like a massively outnumbered samurai who'd lost his sword.

The mental vision made me snicker softly into the near-darkness.

But no, as tempting as that was, I wanted to confront Rudy on my own. Let him face my squirrely wrath. That way, if he tried to pull this kind of crap again, I'd feel entirely comfortable going to the police.

In hindsight, I probably shouldn't have deleted his e-mails, but I was sure some computer genius could resurrect them.

I heard, rather than saw, Curtis. "Still there," he murmured, and I nodded my thanks for the update.

I eased down the hall, glad for the carpeting, original and deep red with gold acanthus leaves on the borders, muffling my footsteps despite being a bit threadbare.

The door to the smoking room was open.

I sidled up alongside it—hey, I watch enough cop shows to know how it's done—and turned my head to peer inside.

It was darker there, but I could hear the *beep-beep* of his EMF, could see the red glow like a sniper's beam.

He was in the middle of the room, turning in a slow circle away from me.

I slipped into the room, and at the same time hit the push-button light switch by the door and shouted "What the hell are you doing in my hotel?"

It had the desired effect, one that I would savor for a good long time.

He yelled, and his EMF meter went flying in one direction as he spun around, arms pinwheeling. The only thing that would have made it more perfect would be if his glasses were askew, but alas, he wasn't wearing any.

Real life is distressingly not like the movies sometimes.

"Hey!" he said. "I—I'm not stealing anything, I swear!"

"Who are you?" I demanded. One thing I *have* learned from movies is to keep the perp talking, get him to confess. Don't admit you already know anything.

"Rudy—Rudy Schwabach. I've e-mailed you—"

I held up my phone. "I'm calling the cops."

"No—no, wait! I haven't touched anything, I swear. Please."

I lowered the phone, considered him. He wasn't as geeky as I'd expected. Thick black hair with a cowlick, kind of a beaky nose, but despite the panic in them, his eyes were a nice shade of brown.

He was taller than me, but then, many people are.

"You broke into my hotel," I said. "Why *shouldn't* I have you arrested?"

"I didn't damage anything, I swear," he said. "If I did, I'll pay for it, honest."

"What are you doing here?"

"You wouldn't answer my e-mails, so I..." He looked down, saw the broken bits of his EMF on the Oriental carpet, bits of black plastic and wiring on the muted blues and greens. He made a sad noise and bent to pick up the main part with wires dangling from it. The shattered pieces were mostly the casing, but the LED screen had popped out, and the antenna zigzagged.

He sighed. "I'm a paranormal investigator. I'd heard that your hotel was a hotbed of paranormal activity, which is why I asked if I could come in and check it out."

"I remember you now," I said, confident in my acting background, however meager, that I didn't sound like I was lying. "I told you to book a tour like everybody else."

"I know, but I didn't want to come for the premade special effects." His voice got a little high at the end of his sentence. I guessed he was in his early thirties, which is way too old be whiny. Especially for a guy.

"I wanted to experience the hotel in its natural state, without the stuff you do for the tourists," he continued. "It's not a scientific study otherwise."

"You think it's a scientific study now?" I asked, raising an eyebrow. Paris Hilton has her hand-on-hip lean-back; I have my scathing look.

Or bemused look, depending on the situation. There's a subtle difference.

Sam appeared, leaning against the fireplace mantle. He definitely looked bemused. The remains of Rudy's EMF gave a series of forlorn beeps, and he turned it eagerly in the opposite direction, away from Sam.

"Your antenna's busted," I pointed out.

He sighed again and tossed the machine on a Morris chair. "Well, it *was* scientific," he said. "This is highly sensitive and advanced equipment for the detection of electro-magnetic frequencies. Experts in the paranormal field agree that ghosts seem to be able to manipulate those frequencies."

"Uh huh." I laced my voice with a fair amount of skepticism.

"You're the one advertising a haunted hotel," he said. "Do you really believe there are ghosts here?"

Janie, lying on the sofa, gave an elaborate shrug as if to say "Well, do you?"

It was all I could do not to laugh. "What if I do?"

"Then I could prove it for you," Mr. Eager Beaver said.

"Who says I want, or need, proof?"

I wasn't really angry anymore. At least, not much. I was still peeved that he'd broken in, invaded my territory. But now I was having too much fun giving him grief.

"Don't you want to know for sure? I mean, conclusive proof of the existence of spiritual activity here?"

"If I did, maybe I would have actually returned your messages," I pointed out. "I think you're more interested in 'proving' something to yourself."

That's when the thought hit me. Rudy was awfully obsessive about finding ghosts. A lot of ghost hunters actually want to *dis*prove the idea, but Rudy sounded like he was all about really hunting them down.

And if he was hunting them, couldn't he be doing something that made them go away? What if he had done something to...

Holy freaking crap.

"Schwabach," I said. "Any relation to Aaron Schwabach, who used to work as a caretaker at the Holly-wood Forever Cemetery?"

The blood drained from Rudy's face. "How did you know that?" he whispered.

"Let's just say a little ghost told me."

His lips tightened. "I don't believe you."

"Okay," I said, because I was rapidly becoming bored with the situation. I was also starting to feel tired. A girl needs her beauty sleep. "That's up to you. Right now, though, it's time for you to leave."

He opened his mouth to protest, and I poked him in the chest. "Leave, or I call the police. Your choice."

He sighed, a big, heaving sigh that intimated I had crushed his very soul. He grabbed his backpack, stuffed the pieces of the EMF into it (I'd have to vacuum the rug tomorrow to get the little bits). He retrieved another small device from the credenza that served as a wet bar, added that to his bulging pack.

I narrowed my eyes. "Have you set up equipment anywhere else in the hotel?"

"No," he said. Then, "No, I *swear!*" in a nervous squeak when I took a step towards him.

I had no idea I could be that scary. I was rather pleased with myself.

"I'd better not find any," I said, and made a mental note to do some sort of sweep. Not that I had any idea how. Daddy had hired security before; maybe they could give me some tips.

But I was pretty sure Rudy was telling the truth. He just didn't strike me as the type to be that sneaky—or that organized, even.

I turned off the lights in the smoking room and switched on my little flashlight. The switches for the foyer lights were on the wall by the front door—old hotel, remember?—and I was too lazy to go all the way over there. Between the flashlight and the streetlights' glow, there was enough for Rudy to see his way to the front door.

I followed him closely. Not that I expected him to bolt. I was just still enjoying being menacing. He wisely didn't say anything, and stepped aside to let me unlock the door.

The first thing I noticed was the air: nice and cool, even compared to the air conditioning inside, and the water in the fountain gave the small courtyard a hint of moisture. In the desert of LA, it's noticeable.

The second thing I noticed was the gate at the other end of the courtyard, leading to the street: it was swinging shut, as if someone had just come in—or snuck out.

I swore I'd locked it before I left this afternoon. And Solange would've gone out the kitchen door after she'd finished tidying up.

Abandoning Rudy (what was he going to do—go back into the hotel?), I dashed around the fountain and burst through the gate.

I expected to tackle some crony of Rudy's, or maybe a homeless person who'd been looking for a place to crash until they saw the flashlight inside.

(In very great hindsight, it was a stupid thing to do, because the person also could have been an armed robber, or high, or crazy, and I *still* didn't have a sword. Although I did have my very dangerous little flashlight.)

I did not expect to bodily crash into Solange.

It was, in fact, probably the last thing I expected.

NINE

FOR A MOMENT I FLAILED, caught in the folds of Solange's voluminous clothing and her signature scent and my own confusion.

She set me back on my feet, holding me out at arm's length. "You nearly scared the life out of me, *cher*!"

"How do you think I feel?" I asked when I was able to gulp in enough air. My heart thudded behind my breast-bone. "What are you *doing* here?"

"I have been searching *all over* for my Kindle, and I thought maybe it had dropped out of my purse here," she said. "I figured you were off with your mama and papa, so I'd just swing by and look for it. You know me, I'm just a night owl anyway."

It was true. I really didn't have any idea when Solange actually slept. I wished she would teach me that trick; I could get sooo much done if it weren't for those pesky nine hours. (When I could get them, that is. Tonight wasn't going to be one of those nights.)

Traffic still steadily swished by on Wilshire; it never really went away, although by this time of night, it wasn't bumper-to-bumper. Nobody would give us a second glance, though.

The headlights and shadows were probably why I thought the gate had moved.

"I haven't seen your Kindle," I said. "Do you want to come inside and look?"

"Oh, no, *cher*, I don't want to bother you. Are you okay? Why are you home? And who's this?"

I turned to see Rudy coming up behind me. Funny, I would've thought he'd've headed in the opposite direction as fast as humanly possible. Maybe I hadn't been as menacing as I'd thought. Phoo.

"This is Rudy, who broke into my home because he wanted to party with the spirits," I said. I didn't introduce him to Solange.

"I did not want to par—"

I glared, and he shut up, and I tried not to feel too smug.

"And he was just leaving," I said.

"Right, yes I was," he said. "Good night, ladies." He even sketched a short bow before jogging off past Solange. I wondered if his car was a hearse with a logo, and was kinda bummed I wouldn't find out.

"You sure you don't want to come in?" I asked.

"*Cher*, you look exhausted," Solange said. "You'll tell me the whole story on Sunday—this Rudy person, the premiere, everything. We'll make popcorn and have a girls' night."

"Let's watch the AAMies," I said, referring to the American Action Movie Awards. "I'll bring Krispy Kremes." Which sounded really good right now, despite how tired I was. What time was it, anyway?

We hugged goodnight, and I locked the gate behind me.

Then I went inside, locked the Ballington's front door, and headed to the smoking room again.

I went back to the smoking room and poured two fingers of whisky into a cut crystal glass. Sam became solid enough to pour himself one as well.

I knocked it back, grimacing as it went down (isn't that a cliché?), then called out, "Staff meeting, smoking room, please!"

Sam and Janie were already in the room, Maggie, my little limpet, had been with me the entire time. Curtis filtered in, headphones dangling around his neck, and finally Marla appeared, timidly. I would've hugged her reassuringly if I could've.

I lay on the floor with my feet up on the sofa, where Janie lounged. I noticed then that my Vans didn't match. In my haste to get over here, I'd grabbed one that was black with pink skulls and crossbones, and one red-and-black checkered. Thank God there were no paparazzi around to catch *that* little gaffe. It couldn't even be excused as trendy or daring fashion, because they simply clashed.

Badly.

Sam slugged back his own drink so he could go incorporeal again, and settled into an armchair. Marla paced behind the sofa. Curtis flopped into another armchair, sitting sideways with his legs hanging over one arm. If he'd been corporeal, I would have had a heart attack that he'd break the antique furniture.

Sometimes I don't know who I am anymore.

Onwards. As unsettled as I was, I felt a certain solace now, surrounded by my friends. I was more comfortable here than I'd been at the after-premiere party. As fun as that had been, here nobody cared about my mismatched shoes.

Well, I did, just a little, but that was beside the point.

"Anybody know how the squirrely little bastard got in?" I asked.

Nobody had a clue, and I mentally kicked myself for not thinking to ask Rudy.

I was *so* going to research getting an alarm system installed tomorrow. Er, today. The first greying of dawn was visible outside the window. I yawned, but there was more we had to discuss.

I sat up, leaned back against the sofa. "Guys, I said, "I'm a little worried about something, and I'm not sure if I should be more worried."

Out of the corner of my eye, I saw Janie sit up on the sofa and lean towards me. I was grateful she took care not to actually touch me. Brrr. Marla stopped her pacing. Curtis cocked his head, and Sam went still.

"Aaron Schwabach, who was my go-to at Hollywood Forever, wasn't there when I took the tour there yesterday," I said. "Then tonight I checked on Thomas and Bertha at the El Capitan, since I was there anyway, and they're gone, too. I told Marilyn about Aaron, and she hadn't hear anything. Have you guys?"

"Oh dear," Janie said. "Do you think something happened to them?"

I shrugged one shoulder. "I never thought Aaron would leave without letting me know. Plus he loved the cemetery. As for Thomas and Bertha, they had each other, so they could have decided to move on..."

"I haven't heard anything," Curtis said.

"Me neither," said Marla. "Should we be worried?"

It was Sam who answered. "Something might have happened to Aaron, but it's just as likely someone he was waiting for finally passed on. Didn't that young man who broke in tonight say he was Aaron's grandson?"

"Which may or may not be a weird coincidence," I said. "But please be careful; keep an eye out, okay? Just in case."

I rubbed my temples. I was normally a night owl, but since I'd stopped my partying ways and started focusing on the hotel, I wasn't used to nights that went *this* late. I climbed to my feet.

"I'm beat," I said. "Thank you, thank you, thank you all: Curtis, for calling me, and everyone for keeping an eye on Rudy. He shouldn't be bothering us again. I'm going to bed. If anything untoward happens, come and get me. Yes, you can come into my room, but only if it's an emergency. Otherwise, I'm exhausted. You all have a good night."

I didn't tell them to sleep well, because I didn't know if ghosts slept, and I'd never thought it polite to ask.

Even Maggie filtered away. The only time she leaves my side is when I'm sleeping. Or maybe she's there, and I just don't see her.

I SHOULD'VE KNOWN BETTER than to tell the ghosts not to disturb me. I should've asked one of them to check on me.

I slept through my alarm, slept through what normal people call breakfast time *and* brunch, slept until what lazy people call lunchtime.

I could've *died* before any of them thought to check on me.

In fact, when I stumbled into the kitchen and found Janie there, I grumbled words to that effect.

"You said 'anything untoward'," she said patiently. "You said 'emergency'. We didn't realize that meant your alarm going off for an hour."

I decided not to argue with her, in large part because she'd somehow known to turn on the coffee maker just before I'd come down. (I'm going to assume someone heard the toilet flush, not that any of them had been lurking in my room watching me.)

I did thank her for the coffee thing. I'm not a monster.

I leaned on the stainless steel island and rubbed my temples. I had a too-much-sleep hangover. The coffee and food would help.

Taking a hefty swig of coffee, I checked in the fridge, and found leftover scones and lemon curd and clotted cream, along with some cheddar and Branston pickle crustless finger sandwiches. *Score.* I'd hit In-N-Out for protein on the way to my parents' house, but that had been several lifetimes ago.

My purse was on the counter next to the fridge where I'd dropped it last night in my haste to confront the intruder. As I shoved it out of the way, I discovered I'd dropped it on top of Solange's missing Kindle.

I popped her a text and let her know I'd bring it by the shop where she worked later this afternoon. Because, conveniently, the shop was near somewhere else I needed to go.

Somewhere where there was someone who might be able to give me some answers about what was going on with the missing ghosts.

If I was willing to pay the cost.

TEN

I HOPPED onto Pacific Avenue and headed north to Santa Monica.

Specifically, the Pier.

Curtis would be pissed that I hadn't told him I was coming here, since one of his favorite movies, *The Lost Boys* (starring his peeps the Coreys) had been filmed here. But I hadn't really wanted to dawdle. I had a goal.

A goal that made me a little bit nervous. Okay, a fair amount of nervous.

The Pier was crowded as usual on a weekend, but I scored and was able to park in the lot on the Pier itself, my car tires rumbling over the wooden slats. As I got out of the car, the wind tossed over to me the faint shrieks of riders on the roller coaster, the Sea Dragon, and the drop tower.

At least, I didn't think they were screaming on the carousel or Ferris wheel. But you never know.

Seagulls swooped low, hoping for a handout or at least a misplaced french fry, as I passed the gift shops and turned left into the amusement park. I was a little hungry—my late lunch felt like a long time ago—but the smell of cotton candy and popcorn didn't sit well with me.

Real food. Later.

I bought tickets, and stood in line for the roller coaster.

The West Coaster isn't known for its height, velocity, or any of those newfangled loops and twists. You didn't ride it for the visceral thrill. You rode it for its history, for its unique status as the only steel roller coaster on a pier over the Pacific. You rode it because it encircled the park, and when you were at the top you could see the Santa Monica Bay and the Pacific Ocean, and they were very pretty.

Or, if you were me, you rode it because there was someone you needed to talk to.

The operator pointed me to a single seat near the back, which I would've happily taken under other circumstances. I love roller coasters almost as much as I love surfing, and I know the last car is the place to be—by the time you tip over the edge, the momentum and speed put you in the perfect spot for weightlessness.

Instead, I selected a seat in the middle. I felt a sudden pang of loss, a clear vulnerability, as Maggie stepped away to stand under a crossbeam, shaking her head.

I don't know if she didn't like coasters or whether she knew she was technically way too short to go on the ride.

Most likely, because she knew there wasn't a seat for her.

I carefully stepped over the inner seat to settle into the outer one.

Ever notice on a lot of roller coasters that there's one seat nobody ever sits in? Even when they've got single riders (when a group doesn't divide evenly), they'll direct people away from a particular seat. It's not even conscious, because sometimes I've asked.

That seat, my friends, is more often than not already occupied.

Because I'm far from the first roller coaster aficionado in the world, and what better place to spend eternity than with your stomach lurching but never actually needing to throw up?

The safety bar came down. "Hey, Otter," I said.

"Hey," said the guy in the "empty" seat next to me.

I could never get a bead on Otter's decade. He wore faded jeans with the beginnings of a hole in the right knee, a blue denim button-down shirt over a red T-shirt, and tennis shoes. Ghosts can't change their clothes, but sometimes I got the sense that this wasn't Otter's original outfit.

Looks-wise, he was of indeterminate age, somewhere between his mid-twenties and his mid-forties, I'd guess. Brown hair that needed a trim, not long or short, just messy.

The West Coaster's only been here since 1996, but there had been a series of coasters here since 1915. That's a big span of time.

I also couldn't tell from his language or slang. Every year he had something new in his vocabulary from listening to all the tourists.

The other thing about Otter? He had his finger on the pulse of the ghost community of Los Angeles. He was sort of the granddaddy, sort of the head of the ghost mafia, maybe, kinda? I don't know how he did it exactly, because he always seemed to be here. I guess he's convinced other spirits to drop by and feed him news. Somehow, he has The Information.

Like I said, his looks were average...except for his eyes.

There was a hint, a glint of silver in them, something deeper than iris and pupil and cornea.

Makes me wonder if he's sticking around for some reason a lot older than a cheesy roller coaster.

I don't know why he's called Otter. Fact is, I know less about Otter than I know about any other ghost I've met. Not for lack of interest, though. He's just not willing to share.

It's like, the only way he'll give information is if you give him some. A trade, like for like. Kind of like in the fairy tales Grandma Rosa used to read to me when I was little. Not the nice fairies, I mean. Like with the real fairies, if you don't have information, I imagine Otter will take something else in pay.

I don't want to know what that might be.

A part of me was scared spitless to even ask him what I needed to ask him now. All I could hope was that I'd be giving him new information first.

The coaster started with a lurch and a rattle.

"I'm worried, Otter," I said over the noise.

"Oh?" He didn't look at me. He gazed ahead, anticipating, his hands resting loosely on the metal bar that would keep us from going airborne.

"Do you know—" Wait. I wanted to ask him if he knew Aaron, but that would be asking a question. "There's a ghost, Aaron Schwabach. He worked at the Hollywood Forever Cemetery, stuck around after he died. Nice guy."

We started up the incline, slow and inexorable. The kids in the car in front squealed, and the sound traveled from rider to rider like an audible wave.

"I know Aaron," Otter said.

He'd given me information, but I hadn't exactly asked for it. I hoped I was safe.

I really wish I'd listened harder to those stories of Grandma Rosa's.

"He'd been helping me with my tour—you're still okay about my tours, right?"

Otter nodded. We'd discussed my tours early on, and I'd had to assure him I wasn't exploiting any ghosts. I asked their permission, warned them ahead of time when I'd be swinging by with my vanload of tourists. Hell, I'd offered all of them compensation, but none of us could come up with anything any of the ghosts actually needed.

"Well, I had a tour yesterday, and—"

We pitched over the edge then. My stomach flew past my head, and I was struck with a fit of hysterical giggles.

I've never been much of a screamer where coasters are concerned.

I waited until everyone else's shrieks had died down a little and we were whipping around a corner to shout, "—and Aaron was missing. Gone. And then I couldn't find Thomas and Bertha at the El Capitan. Have you heard... I mean, I just wanted to let you know, because I was worried about them all."

Otter didn't reply, didn't even look at me. Eyes ahead, he moved with the roller coaster, knowing the car's every move, every tilt and turn. He was like a rider on a familiar horse, one with the beast beneath him.

I don't like this kind of silence. Hate it, in fact. And though there were shrieks and laughter and the hammering noise of the coaster on its tracks, Otter's failure to speak made me feel like I was in a vacuum.

Surrounded by people, but alone.

My therapist has a lot to say about this, none of which really helps.

The bar was slick beneath my palms, but not from any nerves about the coaster.

I closed my eyes, feeling the wind whip by my face,

tangle my hair. Happy place, Nikki, remember? Although in many ways, this was already pretty close to my happy place.

Otter would respond.

Even if I didn't like his response, it would be something.

And I didn't think I'd said anything to lock me in to having to give him my firstborn child if, God forbid, that ever happened. Unlike the Real Teen Housewives, I know better than to start early. I've got shit to do first.

Anyway.

The coaster came into its final stretch and slowed jerkily down. I opened my eyes again, the sunlight harsh even veiled by my sunglasses.

The bar raised, freeing us. People poured off the roller coaster, laughing and talking.

Otter stood and stepped out of the car, then turned and held out his hand to me.

I...what?

Otter *never* got off the roller coaster. He was always *here*. This is where you came to *find* him.

"Lady!" the operator shouted, jolting me out of my shock. "If you want to ride again, you gotta get off and go to the end of the line!"

The line wasn't *that* long, but he had Rules to follow. And I had no interest in pulling out the "But I'm Nikki Ashburne" card, because I didn't want to ride the coaster again, anyway.

At least, not right now.

So because I didn't know what else to do, because I'd been so *thrown* by what just happened that I didn't even think how stupid this would look to people who couldn't see him, I stood and took Otter's hand and stepped up onto the platform next to him.

He let go of my hand, and I immediately covered it with my right, smashing it against my stomach in an effort to warm it back up after a contact that had chilled my fingers to the literal bone.

"Thank you, Nikki Elizabeth Ashburne," he said. "I appreciate your concern about Aaron Schwabach and the others, and that you came here to tell me the news. I recommend that you seek out Tabitha St. Claire. I will let you know what I discover, and I'm certain you'll do the same for me."

Before I could open my mouth to thank *him*, he was gone. Poof, just like that.

"Ma'am..." the operator said. The last stragglers sent strange glances back at me over their shoulders, hesitating with that look of *We don't want to have to help pacify the crazy lady*.

"I'm sorry," I said, and flashed the operator a conciliatory smile. "Just a little woozy. I'll be fine."

I walked down the ramp, Maggie safely back at my side.

I hadn't learned anything, and yet I felt like my whole world had shifted sideways half a step. No wonder I was staggering.

ELEVEN

THE SHOP WHERE SOLANGE WORKED, Star Dust, was in Venice Beach on the promenade, home to tourists and bodybuilders and frequently celebrities. Even though the owner, Bridget, is more serious than the typical palm reader you'd find there, the location, however clichéd, was good for business.

I had to park along one of the canals Venice Beach is famous for; I'd probably get a ticket, but there you have it. The beach was hopping, and I wished I'd brought my board, even though the best surfing is in the early morning. Just one or two hits in the waves would have sufficed, really.

I'm not a drug addict. But riding the surf…does that count as an addiction? I certainly crave it, especially when I'm stressed, like I was now, worried and wondering why ghosts were disappearing.

Even as I tried to shake it off, one part of my brain was analyzing the waves. But I had more important things to engage the main portion of my brain right now.

Ducks paddled in the canal as I made my way past houses of celebrities I knew and didn't know.

Once on the boardwalk, it was a short jaunt to Star Dust.

Despite the breeze from the ocean, it was another scorching LA day, so I was grateful for the air conditioning when I slipped inside. I breathed in Nag Champa incense, a scent that always makes me think of Solange.

The shop sold the usual assortment of goods for any pagan-based faith—Wicca, Druid, Norse, Celtic, Greco-Roman, Voudon, etc.—plus some Hindu items, a few Christian things that might interest the Cult of Mary types, even a smattering of Church of Satan stuff.

Leather-bound blank books for journals or Books of Spells, etched and gilded with designs. Athames, wands, brooms, chalices, statues and figurines, incense, holy water, sage smudges, dried herbs, Tarot and divination cards, crystals...there was a bit of everything here. Not a lot of books; Solange says the Internet pretty much killed that aspect of retail.

Although there was no bell that jingled over the door, or any other sound of my entrance, Bridget, behind the front counter, looked up. The smile to welcome a customer didn't waver when she saw me, but something in her expression changed, making me feel decidedly less welcome.

Gorgeous, magickal Bridget, whom I suspected hated my ever-living guts.

Okay. Maybe that was exaggerating. But I'd already had to deal with enough people who didn't like me lately.

I wasn't exactly sure why Bridget was so entirely frosty towards me. At first I suspected it had something to do with my former life; that she looked down on me, and maybe expected me to one day return to it without a backwards glance, ditching Solange without a second thought.

Hah. As if. But I couldn't convince Bridget of that, and

frankly, I didn't feel the need to waste the energy trying. She'd formed her opinion of me, and that was that.

Bridget was a voluptuous, ringletted redhead Amazon who looked like an Irish goddess and cast a mean I Ching. She used to work as a model years ago, including high-end bondage gear and other such edgy stuff, which is how she raked in the cash to buy a store in this prime real estate.

"Hello, Nikki." Bridget looked awesome as usual. She was wearing a green leather bustier-vest that made her ample charms look particularly ample, with a matching D-ring-studded collar. Below she had on a flowing, patterned skirt with swirls of matching greens and many other colors that somehow went together. I couldn't see much past her waist, but given her stature, she was probably wasn't wearing heels. She didn't need them.

"Hi," I said. "How's business today?" There were four or five people in the store besides us.

"Off and on," she said. "On a day like this, most people are focused on the beach. But eventually they wander in. I'll tell Solange you're here."

"Thanks."

She ducked behind the spiral-printed sheer fabric hanging between the front of the shop and the back rooms, which included a small storeroom, Bridget's office, and a room for Tarot and palm readings and other psychic divination. Solange says a ghost hangs out in the back, but I've never seen him or her. Guess s/he's shy.

Solange emerged a moment later.

For the tour groups, she wore flowing, brightly colored clothes that accentuated her New Orleans heritage. Now she wore an outfit in line with her usual style: formfitting designer jeans and sandals with four-inch heels that brought her almost to Bridget's height. Today she'd paired that with a one-shouldered rust-colored silk top with delicate gold embroidery, a handful of slinky gold chains, and diamond studs.

Damn, but she looked good.

I felt almost frumpy in comparison, which was saying something. I had on a sleeveless Breton striped shirt and white shorts, along with matching navy sandals.

"Nikki!" she cried when she released me. "Thank you so much for swinging by." She leaned in conspiratorially. "I saw you in the celebrity news online this morning. Great dress—and I loved the eyeshadow. Way to make an entrance!"

Oh God, that was right. I'd practically forgotten. The premiere felt like it had been weeks ago. By tonight the entertainment programs would be airing their pieces about the premiere, but the Internet would have already covered it.

I reminded myself to stay offline for a day or two.

I'd break that promise by this evening, probably, but it's good to have goals, you know?

"Thanks," I said. "I felt pretty damn good, too." At least until Evan ignored me, and I discovered Thomas and Bertha were gone, et cetera.

As I fished her Kindle out of my bag and handed it to her, I realized I hadn't told Solange about Aaron, much less the others. We were going to get together tomorrow night anyway, but because this disturbing weirdness was my focus right now, she (and the next person I'd be visiting) was a good resource. I glanced around. Bridget was still in the back. Good. I had never told her outright about my ghost-interacting abilities, although she may have figured something out or Solange might have let something slip. I didn't care much either way, but I didn't want to announce it now, either.

"Changing the subject entirely," I said, "have you heard anything about ghosts disappearing?"

Solange's eyes, surrounded by dramatic eyeliner, widened, and her nostrils flared. "I haven't. What's going on? Who's gone?"

"Aaron Schwabach at Hollywood Forever, and Thomas and Bertha at the El Capitan," I said. "Marilyn hasn't heard anything, either, and Otter..."

"You spoke to Otter?" Solange's voice was sharp. "Did he tell you anything else?" she asked.

"Nope. Cryptic as usual. I think I escaped with my soul intact."

Solange was quiet. Then, finally, she chuckled, as if realizing I'd made a joke. "Maybe..." she hesitated. "Maybe Aaron and the others decided it was just time? Occam's Razor?"

"What?"

"Sometimes the simplest explanation is the right one," she said.

Oh. Okay. "Thomas and Bertha, maybe. But Aaron was happy here. He'd chosen to stay. Why would he suddenly change his mind?" And not tell anybody? I wanted to add.

Admittedly, it wasn't as if we were close. Hung out, chatted. He'd agreed to be a part of my tour, thought it was a gas.

But he never revealed that much about himself. We weren't BFFs.

For example, he'd never told me about Rudy.

She shrugged. "There are probably any number of reasons," she said. "People get tired, change their surroundings all the time. Hell, every time I get bored, I do something crazy with my hair."

It was currently in a big bun, with a flower in it. Very chic. Not crazy at all.

"Yeah, but it seems like a pretty big step," I said. "Hair grows back, or you can get extensions. Leaving this plane for good...that's permanent."

"Had he said anything? Acted any differently recently?"

I shook my head. "Not that I'd noticed. He knew I had a tour group coming through yesterday," I added. "He's one of the most conscientious people I've ever met. He would have warned me, not left me in the lurch."

Solange frowned. "I hadn't thought of that," she murmured, half to herself.

"My guys don't know anything," I said, referring to my friends at the Ballington. "Sam's doing some checking, though. Handy to have a detective."

"Are all of your crew okay?" she asked. "Are any of them here?"

"Just Maggie's with me, and yes, they're all fine."

Solange gazed into the middle distance, slightly upwards. "Hello, Maggie," she said. "You're always welcome here."

I never quite understood why she didn't look at Maggie or the rest of the ghosts directly, but I guess it was her thing. She was a medium, more used to channeling spirits, interacting with them differently than I did. Maggie was plain to me, perched on the counter, her legs swinging back and forth.

"If it was Aaron's decision, why would my friends be in trouble?" Sometimes Solange leaps a little too far ahead for me.

It was her turn to shake her head. "Sorry. Pondering multiple possibilities. Maybe Aaron doesn't want to be found, or followed."

"I'm pretty sure he's completely gone, not just hiding or moved," I said.

"Just in case…"

"True. I'll let Sam know." I still though it was a long shot, but hey, I was no expert. I was just worried about my friends.

I sipped my coffee. It was cooling, but it still tasted awesome.

"I'll contact my spirit guide," Solange said. "After I close up shop tonight. See if she knows anything. But really, the simplest answer is the best answer. We know that most ghosts stick around because they just don't want to move on for some mundane reason. Aaron probably found a reason to ascend."

"Maybe," I said doubtfully. It just didn't make sense. She didn't know Aaron like I did—she didn't really know Aaron at all, in fact. She'd never been to the cemetery with me.

But I didn't want to argue, either. "I doubt it, but I'll keep that in mind," I said. "I can't say what might have changed for Thomas and Bertha, but they didn't seem the type."

Aaron hadn't told me much about his former life, but I'd talked more with Marla, Janie, Sam, and Curtis. They all have a different reason for being here, but all the explanations sort of boil down to attrition. They still like it here, even if they can't interact on the same levels they did when they were alive.

Some people get weary of the world. I imagine it's a great comfort to be given that option to move on to some place that's...I don't know, quieter. Not just outside noise, but inside noise as well.

Inner peace. Leave your cares behind.

But wouldn't it be cool to stick around, hang out at your favorite places, and watch how the world changes? To get a sense of all the cycles well past what you'd be able to observe in a single lifetime?

To make fun of all the new fashions, especially when they're just rehashes of the old ones? (Don't get me started on hairstyles.) Or, since ghosts are stuck in the clothes they died in (think about that before you leave the house today), to enjoy the new fashions vicariously.

"Knocking them off the list for a moment, then you're only talking about Aaron's disappearance as suspicious," Solange said. "I know he was conscientious, *cher*, but if something made him want to go, he might have just been too intent and focused to remember to tell you."

"Well, I appreciate you asking around," I said.

"I'll see what I can find out," she promised, and hugged me again, surrounding me with her earthy incense scent.

I PAUSED to adjust to the heat outside when I heard a voice call "Nikki!"

Not in a friend-hailing-you kind of way. No, this tone was all too familiar. It was the cry of "Celebrity, look over here!"

I didn't have to glance down to know Maggie was with me. I was safe from cameras, at least, and it had been a looooong time since anyone tried to ambush me.

Since I'd also half-recognized the voice, I wasn't at all surprised to see Donny sitting on a wrought-iron-and-wood bench by the edge of the boardwalk, camera around his neck.

"Consulting a psychic again, eh?" he called over.

I wandered across the cement walkway. "She's not a psychic," I said. "Well, yes, she is, but she's not reading my palm or anything. She's a friend."

I suppose, technically, I had been consulting her. Semantics. Bite me.

"Interesting choice of friends," he said. He squinted up at me, shading his eyes with his hand, and tilted his head a little so the sun was directly behind me and not glaring in his eyes.

"D'ya think?" I dropped onto the bench beside him. "Some people seeing us talking all the time might think you and I are friends, and an interesting choice at that."

"Ah, Nikki, if you were truly my friend, you'd let me get some juicy shots of you, let me make some serious money." He was grinning, his voice playful.

It's not like we hadn't had this discussion before.

"Living in an empty hotel isn't enough?" I asked. "Spending mysterious amounts of time with a psychic? I give and give and give."

"At least you haven't given your secret of how you mess up my photos to the celebrity world," he said. "That would ruin every photographer's career."

"Well," I said, "I hope you won't be disappointed waiting forever." I stood. "You following me to my car?"

"Nah." He turned and looked out over the beach. "I might be able to catch someone here. I heard Asia McBride might be by."

As I walked along the canals, I thought about the irony of what he'd said. He wanted me to do something really interesting.

Good thing he didn't know that I talked to ghosts.

That reminded me of the whole problem again. I paused and tapped my fingernails on the wooden railing separating the sidewalk from the water below. I didn't want to have to wait until tomorrow to hear from Solange, but I had no choice.

It was only after I was back at my car that I realized I'd forgotten to tell Solange about Rudy being Aaron Schwartz's grandson. I was beginning to think it was just an extremely freaky coincidence, anyway.

Wasn't it?

TWELVE

WHO THE HELL was Tabitha St. Claire?

Before I searched for the answer to that, though, food was a priority.

I went to my favorite sushi place, a little dive in a strip mall. It used to be a Mexican place, and still retains the orangey-red Formica tables and a wallpaper border of dancing peppers. The new owners have made a halfhearted effort to hang some Asian paper banners around and play traditional music (or at least music that sounded that way to me), but they focused on the fish, and that was what was important.

It was midafternoon, so the place was far from crowded, but there was a couple in a red booth, their plates long cleared away, who were nursing their drinks, holding hands, and staring soulfully at each other, and a group of retired-age people holding down the fort on the other side of the small room.

I took a seat on a black padded stool with a back rest at the end of the bar in the back. The glass-fronted bar gave me a view of the fish and rice and seaweed wrappers. I asked the chef—who knew me—for whatever was good that day, however he wanted to make it. That, my friends, is the best way to get the best sushi. Respect the chef.

While I waited, I pulled out my phone and fired up the Googles, and searched for Tabitha St. Claire.

Thankfully, she'd been someone famous. Otherwise, I'd've been lost. If it's not on the Internet, forget about it.

What the all-mighty, blessed Internet had to say about her was this:

Tabitha St. Claire had been an actress, with most of her work in the late 1930s and early 1940s. She was a statuesque, swanky, husky-voiced brunette—glamorous, curvaceous, flirtatious. The camera had loved her.

So, it seemed, had her peers.

By all accounts, she threw a hell of a party, and loved every minute of it. Champagne fountains, show girls, imported delicacies...you name it, she had it. Her Mardi Gras party involved masquerades from Italy, and if it was your birthday, well, fireworks were just the beginning.

She was a regular on the party circuit, too. You *wanted* her at your parties, because she turned them into something special.

Well, go Tabitha.

Then, somehow—and nobody was quite clear on how or why—things went south.

The chef smiled and handed me a plate of salmon and ahi artfully draped over rice and rolled with other nummy things. I freed my chopsticks from their paper, poured soy sauce into the little rectangular bowl, and dug in.

Tabitha's career plummet could have been the excessive partying affecting her acting career, physically or mentally, so the parts dried up. It could have been that she fell out of favor—God knows, that happens in a heartbeat in Hollywood. It could have been that she couldn't gracefully age and accept roles that didn't involve sexy temptresses.

Whatever the cause, her friends moved on. The party invitations petered out. The acceptances to her soirees, ditto.

Undoubtedly, also the money. Which led back to both the lack of throwing exorbitant parties as well as the ability to be fabulous and fashionable and stunning at parties.

Jaysus. There but for the grace of God go I, as they say.

The crowning blow was when she arranged a lavish, over-the-top party for her own birthday, and pretty much nobody RSVP'd in the affirmative.

To add insult to injury, her competition was holding a party that night, one that everybody who was anybody was going to, and Tabitha hadn't been invited.

At the last minute, she was. As an obvious afterthought. Out of pity.

She put on her most stunning satin gown, the last of her glittering, sumptuous diamonds. She ensured her hair and makeup were exquisite. She arrived in a rented (and never paid for) limousine.

She swept in, called everyone to her...

...and dramatically (and no doubt utterly gracefully) dropped dead at their feet.

There were no drugs in her system. Not a drop of alcohol. She'd simply made her final spectacular entrance, and then an exit nobody would soon forget.

I wiped soy sauce from the corner of my mouth with a napkin and drummed my still impressively manicured fingers on the table.

What a story. What a life.

What a death.

Tabitha St. Claire hadn't died happy. She couldn't even

be said to have died contented. So why hadn't she moved on? Why was she sticking around? From my admittedly limited experience, people who'd been unhappy in life were *more* likely to move on, to find something better that what they'd experienced here.

Why say "Fuck you, I'm going to ruin your party by dropping dead," then hang around any longer than it took to see the party ruined?

I needed more information than the Googles could provide.

I went back home to the Ballington, to my favorite space: the solarium.

It's a stunning, multi-storied space at the back of the hotel, all big panes of glass separated by sleek Art Deco–patterned, dark green iron. Amber Deco light sconces, which miraculously weren't stolen when the Ballington was closed up, surround the space at the first level. There's a fountain, metal benches, marble statues tucked in amongst the plants. I supply the fertilizer and whatnot, but it's Janie who keeps everything growing. Ironic that someone who's dead is so good at tending living things; even more so because she says when she was alive, she had a brown thumb.

Some things, we just don't question.

"Hey, Sam?" I called into the empty air. "You around?"

A moment later, Sam shimmered into the air next to me, fedora dipped low across one eye.

"How're you doing, Nikki?" he asked. "You had quite a night last night."

I couldn't help but grin. He was so…protective of women.

"We all had a hell of a night," I said. "But I'm doing fine.

Thanks for asking." I indicated the seat next to me on the bench, and with a nod, he sat.

"I'm looking for someone who was alive when you were," I said. "Otter says she's still around, and I should talk to her about what's been going on. Have you ever heard of Tabitha St. Claire?"

I didn't expect Sam's reaction. I was figuring on either yeah, he'd heard of her, or no, not really. More likely the former, since she'd been a relatively well-known actress in his time.

Ghosts don't get pale, the blood doesn't drain on their faces like it happens with the living. They technically don't have blood to drain, you know.

Instead, when they're shocked or upset, they tend to flicker in and out.

For a moment there, I pretty much lost Sam.

I took that to mean the answer to my question was, "Hell, yes."

A little concerned, I waited for Sam to pull himself together. Literally. Okay, I was concerned, but I was also a little punchy. Hee.

I waited, and finally he resolidified—but he didn't look happy.

"Are you okay?" I asked.

He took a deep breath (insofar as he went through the motions, because, you know, ghosts and breathing, not so necessary) and nodded.

"I just didn't expect you to mention Tabby—Tabitha," he said.

Tabby? "You knew her?"

Another nod. "I investigated her death."

"I don't know a lot about it other than what I've just read," I said. "They—you—didn't find any foul play?"

"No evidence, but I've never been convinced."

Iiiinteresting. I wasn't sure if it was worth pursuing now, but one evening soon I'd ply Sam with whisky and get the whole story.

Plus I had a strong sneaking suspicion that there was more to the story than just the fact that he'd investigated her death. He'd called her "Tabby."

He'd known her personally.

He looked like he'd really need the whisky. He was slumped in the chair, turning his hat over and over in his hands. I'd never seen him like this before.

"Otter said she might know what's going on with Aaron Schwabach's disappearance," I said. "Do you know where I can find her?"

"No."

No? WTF?

"I mean, she doesn't stay in one place," Sam clarified, as if realizing how curt and unhelpful he'd sounded.

Well, that was kinda weird. Most of the ghosts I knew did have a regular hangout, someplace that made them happy. Like my friends and this hotel. Marilyn and the Roosevelt. Aaron and the cemetery. The only exception I'd run into was Maggie, and for some reason she'd decided her "place" was with me.

"Is she with someone?" I asked.

"She goes wherever lots of people are," Sam said. "She goes wherever the parties are. Not the clubs or bars, but the...upscale parties."

"Ohhhh. I get it. She's reliving all the bashes she went to when she was alive. That makes sense."

Jaysus. My mother throws some pretty elaborate do's. Had Tabitha been to our house?

Now that was a little spooky, even for me.

"So, Otter thinks she'll have information?" Sam asked.

I thought back to what Otter had said. "He said to seek her out," I said. "So yeah. Any idea where she'd be soon?"

"Wherever the parties are," he said.

It was my turn to nod. "I'll ask my mother," I said. "She'll know."

"I'll see what I can find out as well," Sam said. "And Nikki..."

"Yeah?"

"If you find Tabitha, please don't mention my name."

Holy crap. The rest of this could wait. I'd get him a whisky if he wanted, but everything else could go on hold until I asked him about—

But Sam was gone, without even a goodbye. He was shaken up more than he would ever admit, by the mere mention of one Tabitha St. Claire.

When I found Tabitha, I wouldn't tell her that I knew Sam, but I just might ask if she'd known him. Something had gone on between the two of them—something serious.

Finding Tabitha...that meant finding some big fancy bash. Hang on—hadn't my mother been talking about somebody's fiftieth birthday extravaganza?

I grabbed my phone, called her. She understood the importance of being seen, and if I'd done nothing else to impress her in my life, she'd seen the business sense of how much money I'd made being a presence at clubs and parties.

From zero to sixty in the social scene, that was me.

I hoped I had something suitable to wear. What was the appropriate dress code for meeting with a famous actress? Especially one who'd been dead for decades? There are no etiquette books for this, dammit.

THIRTEEN

THE WAVERLY'S party was a far cry from the ones I used to go to. For one thing, it was a lot quieter, the music being classical rather than hip hop, and coming from muted, hidden speakers rather than subwoofers to make your back teeth shiver. The exquisite canapés were served by white-coated waitstaff, the wine expensive and well-chosen, and the guests dressed to the nines. (Nine *whats*, I've always wondered.)

I felt like an imposter, which is why I'd come with my parents: for vouching purposes.

Plus I'd grown up around the elite of Hollywood and I'd been trained in the social graces of such situations. They might expect me to drink too much and puke in the pot of rare hothouse orchids, but I knew better than that. That was reserved for clubs and beach parties. And other people. I have limits. And I hate to puke.

I was dressed appropriately in a cocktail dress and heels, tasteful makeup, a small diamond necklace and earrings that had been my twenty-first birthday present from my parents (and were the only diamonds I owned).

The Waverlys were old-school Hollywood. Mrs. Waverly was descended from the silent-screen director Harold Kincaid and two generations of award-winning actors. Mr. Waverly's forebears had been railroad magnates and entrepreneurs, not quite as savvy as Getty himself, but well enough to line the family coffers for generations to come.

To that end, if their house wasn't a family home, it very well could have been. I felt a little squee of comfortable familiarity when I saw it. Built in the late 1930s, it was like an older sibling to my Ballington.

It was also, I hoped, the perfect site for Tabitha St. Claire to make an appearance.

I had swung by to visit Marilyn briefly beforehand, to see if she had ever hung out with Tabitha.

She'd met Tabitha once or twice, she said, and thought she was impossibly sad and tragic. (That would have been funny coming from the real Marilyn.) "Just don't mention her death, or the problems leading up to it," Marilyn recommended. "She doesn't like to think about that."

Well, who would? Abandoned by your friends and penniless? Dramatically dropping dead was probably the best thing that could have happened to poor Tabitha.

I made the first round with my parents (oh, the thrills), nibbling on appetizers and sipping a really nice merlot. (*Really* nice. As in, I didn't want to think about the fortune that had been dropped on the alcohol alone for this shindig.) I admired the massive ice sculpture, truly an indulgence in the height of a southern California summer.

I wondered whether the Waverlys had dolphins in their pool, too.

Wouldn't that be cool? When I was a kid, I'd tried to

convince my parents we really, really needed otters in our pool. They'd love the slide, I argued fervently.

My mother had said she was allergic to otters.

Of course, she'd said that about every animal I suggested bringing into our home.

Maybe I should get a couple of cats for the Ballington. Maybe the ghosts could play with them.

But right now, I had a different ghost to find.

No, first I had another, more pressing matter.

The bathroom was all black marble and tall red orchids (See? I knew there'd be orchids) in sleek white pots. I turned on the water as if to wash my hands.

"I have to figure out just how to find Tabitha," I said to Maggie. "I can't just start walking around calling her name. People frown on that sort of thing. Suggest that another 'spa visit' might be in order."

She giggled silently.

"Also, there are so many people here I'm not sure I'd spot a non-living one unless I ran into them and froze my butt off, and people would also frown on me going around and touching everyone to see if they're corporeal. So I'm hoping you can find Tabitha for me."

Maggie nodded, curls bouncing.

I described what Tabitha looked like: elegant and cool, dark brown hair in a '40s coif, probably some kind of gown from the same era.

Maggie nodded again, then filtered away.

I exited the bathroom, raised my glass to my mouth and took a sip, at which point Maggie popped back, startling the hell out of me.

I sputtered the wine back into the glass and glanced around. Nobody seemed to have notice. Small mercies.

Maggie was pointing. I followed her gaze and bam, saw the elusive and tragic Tabitha.

The ghost stood at the top of the curved, sweeping stairs that led down into the foyer. One hand on the bannister, she gazed down at the milling guests below like a queen surveying her realm.

Then she stepped forwards, gliding gracefully down the steps, back straight, shoulders squared, displaying to full effect her stunning mint-green satin halter dress and her diamond choker. Her head was ducked slightly as she surveyed the crowd, her long dark hair carefully formed into waves you could surf on.

Oh yes. Tabitha was all about the grand entrance.

And who could blame her? She was fucking stunning. I was envious of her grace, her untouchable beauty. I'm clumsier than a drunken roller-skating juggler at Venice Beach. (Yes, I've seen that, and yes, it wasn't pretty.) One of my greatest failures is that I can't walk down stairs without looking at them. There are certain awards shows I can never present at because of that.

Tabitha reached the bottom of the stairs, mingled in with the crowd. She eased between people, never touching them, but once she reached out to a passing waiter's tray and trailed her fingers through the crystal champagne flutes, a wistful look on her face.

I didn't blame her.

I understood that look. She was on the outside, unable to get back in to the place she was before. She could attend the party, but she couldn't truly be a part of it.

Yeah. I got that. Totally.

There but for the grace of God go I... I hadn't died at a party. (Well, I had, but I got better.) She hadn't been so lucky—unless, of course, she intended to be that dramatic.

Still, despite the anguish I'd felt last year, I hadn't taken the drugs with the intent to commit suicide.

At the premiere, though, I'd put on a dress that made me feel good and gone back into the limelight, at least to hover on the fringes, and was reminded that the inner circle wasn't where I was welcome anymore, wasn't where I belonged.

And here was Tabitha, doing the same.

She floated out to the patio. I ditched my wine and I grabbed two glasses of champagne—she struck me as champagne woman, or vodka gimlet woman, but champagne was easier—and followed her, Maggie trotting next to me.

The house had been built on the side of a slope in the Hollywood Hills, and only providence (or something disturbing and black magic-y that had been buried in the foundation) had saved it from sliding to its doom during a mudslide or earthquake. It also meant creative landscaping, and the back garden was set on a series of tiers. A stone porch ran the length of the house, overlooking the levels. In the distance twinkled the lights of Los Angeles, not unlike the ones I'd gazed upon on my fateful night.

Tabitha stood at the granite railing, gazing out at those lights. The ones that had embraced her and then cast her aside. I stepped up behind her right shoulder, looking past her. The next level down had a long pool surrounded by groomed plants and tasteful nighttime lighting.

I didn't want to startle her. I eased up to the railing. "Miss St. Claire?"

She turned expectantly (maybe hopefully, which made me feel bad) in a whirl of bias-cut satin skirt and Je Reviens perfume. "Yes?" Then she frowned. "Wait, you're not—" She took a step back. "You're alive. But you can see me?"

I nodded. "I can see ghosts, yes. I'm sorry to bother you, but Otter said you might be able to help me."

"Otter sent you?" A fond smile played on her ultra-red lips. "I haven't spoken to him in...well, far too long. How is he?"

I had no clue how Otter ever was, so I had no frame of reference, but I still said "He's doing fine." Because he'd seemed fine to me, you know.

"Good," she murmured, her thoughts obviously else-where from the distant look in her eyes.

"Miss St. Claire, can we talk?"

"Of course." Her lips curved in a different smile, one she'd probably reserved for photographers in her day. Pleasant enough, but you knew you weren't actually reaching her. It wasn't at all like the one for Otter.

Huh. I wondered how she'd react if I'd mentioned Sam. I'd promised not to, though. If he came up in conversation, well, I couldn't help that. I was dying to know what their interaction had been.

We moved to the left, down the wide steps to the next level of the yard. Another set of stairs led down into a little grotto area with a fountain. I didn't want to think about how much water it took to keep everything lush and green.

All this running water, meanwhile, was making me have to pee again.

I held out one of the glasses of champagne. Her smile broke through her reserve, a sudden burst of warmth and light. I had the strange thought that she should smile more.

"Thank you," she said, and I could tell she meant it. "I'm so sorry. I haven't asked your name."

"Nikki. Nikki Ashburne."

"Ashburne," she said thoughtfully, rolling the name on her tongue as if to spark her memory.

"I don't think you would have known my family," I said. "My father's a well-known producer now, but he would have been a child when...during your heyday," I amended hastily.

"Perhaps I've heard his name since then," she said graciously. "Edward, is it?"

"Yes." Wow. She was really holding on. In that sense she was a lot like Curtis, keeping a finger on the pulse of the new while clinging to the familiar past, wishing it to return but accepting, grudgingly, that it wouldn't.

Or maybe they just clung to the past. What did I know? I was too wrapped up in my own problems.

"So, Nikki Ashburne," she said, touching her glass to mine with a gentle, achingly gorgeous chime that only true crystal can produce, "what can I help you with."

Now that I was here, facing her, I found myself struggling to distill what I needed to say. Way to be prepared, Nikki.

"You know I can see ghosts," I said. "Over the past year, I've gotten to know a few in the area. Aaron Schwabach at Hollywood Forever was one of them. He disappeared a few days ago. No warning, nothing. I didn't get the sense that he'd been planning to cross over; I thought he was happy at the cemetery."

Despite her impeccably applied pale makeup, a pair of fine lines appeared between Tabitha's brows. Those lines had probably been her first sign of mortality, signaling the beginning of the end of her career. Without thinking, I rubbed the area just above my nose.

"I hadn't expected Aaron to move on, either," she admitted. "I haven't spoken to him in so long, though. This is... distressing news."

"I'm sorry that I have to be the one tell you about it," I

said. "The thing is, it looks like he might have been just the first."

Her eyes widened. Damn, I could see why she'd been so sought after. Her expressions were perfectly wrought on her face. And I didn't think she was acting right now.

"Thomas and Bertha at the El Capitan," I said. "They're also gone. I just...I'm worried, and wondering if this is being done to them, against their will."

"Done to them." Tabitha repeated my words. "Somebody is doing this deliberately?"

"That's what I'm trying to find out," I said. "I can't do anything to bring them back, but I want to make sure it stops happening, if it's not by their choice."

"And they were the only ones?"

"The only ones I know about," I said. "But I don't know everyone."

"You seem like the type who would," she said, cocking her head and appraising me with impossibly blue eyes. "Like I was."

"I did, for a while," I said. "Not anymore."

Now those eyes registered sympathy, or maybe empathy. The recognition of a kindred spirit.

"The point is, I've never had that kind of popularity among the ghosts," I went on. "I know quite a few, but I don't see most of them on a regular basis..."

"And you think that I do?" she asked.

"I don't know," I admitted. "I guess that's why Otter sent me to you. He didn't say specifically."

That mysterious smile again. "Well, that's Otter for you."

Well, the whole Otter thing was starting to piss me off. Tabitha hadn't even known this was happening, and she was being as enigmatic as he was.

"So," I said, trying my best not to let my frustrations show, "d'you think you could ask around? See if anybody you know knows anything about what's going on?"

Tabitha tipped back the crystal flute and let the last of the champagne run down her throat. She set the glass in a niche in the grotto; I imagine the Waverly's staff would spend a good portion of tomorrow wandering around the estate collecting errant dishware, like a bizarre Easter egg hunt.

"I will certainly see what I can do," she said, but as she spoke, she was looking past me, back up the stairs at the lights that spilled onto the stone balcony. She wanted— maybe needed—to be back at the party. To be surrounded by people.

To believe, even though they couldn't see her, couldn't interact with her, that they loved her, and that she was a part of their world.

There were so many things I wanted to ask her. Like, was her death accidental? Or had she managed to stage the perfect movie-worthy suicide? Or had nefarious forces been at work?

And did she regret it? Had she learned anything since then that made her understand how she could have better handled her loss of status, her realization that her friends weren't really friends after all?

I knew, though, that now was not the time for those kinds of questions.

"If you think of anything, or hear anything, you'll let me know?" I felt I had to repeat the question that way, to make sure it had sunk in.

"Of course, Nikki." She rested a hand near my arm; it would have been on my arm if it wouldn't have felt like being stabbed with an icicle. "How would I be able to find you?"

"I live at The Ballington Hotel," I said. I was about to add, "Do you know it?" but beneath her pale makeup, Tabitha had gone white as a...sheet. She took a step back.

"The Ballington?" she whispered. "But that's where—"

And then she filtered out of existence, just like Marla did when she was freaked out, when the world got to be too much.

Lingering on the air, though, I thought I heard her voice brokenly murmur, "Sam..."

FOURTEEN

I STAYED at the party a bit longer, nibbling caviar on toast points and imported Turkish figs stuffed with imported Greek cheese wrapped in bacon from pigs probably also imported and fed with caviar, but I was bored.

And I wanted to ask Sam more about Tabitha, no matter how he felt.

And I missed all my friends at the hotel.

When I left, it was still early enough that maybe I could text Solange and she could come over to watch the AAMies like we'd planned. I decided to wait until I got home, because I wasn't sure how it would go with Sam.

Just in case, though, I stopped to pick up a dozen Krispy Kreme donuts.

Original Krispy Kremes are neither krispy nor kremey, but they melt in your mouth like cotton candy for adults. That sugar glaze is better than crack (or so I've been told—I can believe it, though). Oh, and when that light goes on to tell you they're coming out hot off the conveyor belt...well. It's enough to make baby Jesus cry.

The best part was watching the donut-making machine

while you were standing in line, seeing those donuts come marching out on the conveyor belt. I'd been fascinated by that as a kid. Then Ned had gotten a perpetual motion machine for Christmas, and we learned that I could stand in front of it for hours, it seemed, totally mesmerized. We had to get rid of it because it just seemed a little too obsessive for me.

I don't admit that to most people.

At a stoplight, I couldn't stop myself. I popped open the box, fished out a warm one, and indulged. Oh yeah. Baby.

Beside me, Maggie tapped me on the leg—I felt the icy touch and saw her giggling silently. I followed her gaze. In the open Jeep next to me, three young buff guys grinned at my indulgence. For good measure, I made a show of lasciviously licking my lips free of glaze, and while they were all sort of stunned by that, the light turned green and I blasted my little Mini away from them.

Endorphins, caffeine, *and* sugar. Almost as good a high as surfing.

I missed surfing. Some of the shine had been taken off since Ned and I fell apart—I didn't have anyone else to go with, except for the ghost I met that one time, and I didn't think he'd be good backup in an emergency—plus I'd been busy with the hotel and the tours.

Maybe I needed to rectify that. I mentally added it to my never-ending list.

They were doing some road work on my block, bright klieg lights and equipment and a detour around. Finally I pulled into my alley. Donny was waiting at the end by the street. I hopped out and asked him if he wanted a donut.

"You know, you're the only person who offers me food—or pretty much talks to me," he commented as he selected a sugary treat.

"I respect your persistence," I said. "It makes me feel loved and wanted."

"You're a strange woman, Nikki Ashburne."

"You're a stubborn photographer, Donny. 'Night."

I shoved opened the sticky kitchen door (I really needed to fix that), and just managed not to drop the big white box in the process. I was glad to unload a donut on Donny, really. If I ate too many of them on my own, I was going to have to start running stairs. And the Ballington has a *lot* of—

Marla screamed.

I didn't so much *hear* it as *feel* it somehow. It was awful. A vibration in my chest, as if my intestines were being pulled up my throat via my heart.

But Maggie, beside me, did scream aloud. It was the first noise I'd ever heard out of her in the year that she'd shadowed me, and it freaked the holy hell out of me. It was awful, too. Pure terror, like a razor blade slicing through the vibration.

The box of Krispy Kremes fell to the floor. I kicked off my heels and started running.

I didn't know where I was running to. Just to Marla. But where was she? The hotel had a million rooms.

"Marla? Marla! Sam, Janie, Curtis! Dammit, somebody?!"

Maggie filtered out, filtered back, wide-eyed and frantic, like she was going to throw up. She opened her mouth, but she still wouldn't, or couldn't, talk to me.

And dammit, I never could read lips.

I skidded to a stop in the lobby, dimly lit from a few sconces and the streetlight outside coming through the transom.

I didn't know where to go.

"Marla! Dammit, where are you?"

Sam, dear Sam, wavered in front of me, as if in bad movie dream sequence.

"Nikki, hurry!"

"*Where*, dammit?"

I don't think he actually said "Solarium." He was so stressed, so barely there with me, that he didn't have the energy-presence to speak. Instead, I got a vibe, a mental picture, sort of. I saw greenery, ferns, and smelled loamy earth and tasted, of all things, the white wicker bench with the musty-smelling floral-print cushion Janie loved to sit on when she surveyed her lush surroundings.

I saw Marla huddled on that bench, lying in a fetal position, fingers clinging to the cushion as if it were a lifeline. She was shivering in and out, corporeal and then see-through, as if she couldn't maintain her shape.

I'm just a girl who happens to be able to see ghosts, you know? But at that moment, I tried to tell her to hang on, that I was coming.

As if she could hear me, she looked up, her eyes wide and panicked and maybe a little crazy with fear, but also with desperate hope, as if she knew I was coming and trusted me to stop whatever was happening to her. I couldn't hear her, but her lips shaped "Help me." That much I could tell.

It was bad enough.

Heart in my throat, I took off running again.

Sam, Janie, Curtis, and Maggie all stood outside the French doors to the solarium. The doors were leaded, with etched-glass panels in an Art Deco pattern, which through light, but you couldn't see much through them. Sam was pounding on the door, but he wasn't corporeal so he wasn't actually hitting it. But if he was incorporeal, something was wrong, because his fist was still rebounding off of...something.

"We can't get through," Janie said, her voice catching.

Curtis was pale and shaky, and I knew that look: He was jonesing for a hit, and there were no hits to be had. He couldn't escape this.

Something, some kind of weird barrier, was keeping them all from getting through to help Marla.

I, not being a ghost, was not so affected. I grabbed the door handle and yanked hard enough to bust the fragile lock. I didn't even care, at that moment, if I destroyed the nearly 100-year-old glass.

What stopped me wasn't some mystical obstruction, but the scream.

Terror, and resistance, and despair. It was horrifying, and it ripped through me like shattering glass, shredding my gut.

"Marla!"

But even as I stumbled into the solarium, I knew she was gone. Not just off to wherever in the ether ghosts go. *Gone* gone. No more Marla. She'd moved on.

Or, more rightly, been sent on, *forced* on, entirely against her will. Screaming and terrified. Trusting me to save her, and I'd failed.

I wanted to hope that she'd gone somewhere where she'd be happy, with Jim again, but it was hard to believe that. If that existed for her, she would've gone long ago.

I remembered her stretched out on the ground by the bench, absently stroking a fern, wistfully saying blogs were groovy, and I'd promised to help her with one. But I never had. I'd failed her there, too.

I never loved Marla the way I did my grandmother. No slur on Marla; it's just that my grandmother had been a part of me for far longer, such a fixture in my life. But there was something in the loss that was the same. The knowledge that you'd never, ever see that person again.

Ever.

It was almost impossible to comprehend, and when you did, the weight of the world smashed down, drove the breath out of you, and left you so empty you couldn't comprehend how to function.

There's no do-again. It was over. You were alone.

I sank onto the bench and wept and yelled at the universe and kicked over a potted fern, scattering dirt across the tiled floor.

When that didn't work, I called Solange.

I could barely get her name out.

"*Cher*, what's wrong?" she asked, concern sharpening her normally mellow voice, her Creole accent stronger. "Take a deep breath. Ground. Talk to me, honey."

I almost couldn't hear her because of some insane pounding background noise. I managed to convey that between great gulps of air, and I was amazed when she understood me, because I couldn't really comprehend my own words. But the noise faded to a dull background roar.

"Sorry, they're working on the sidewalk outside. Damn jackhammers are giving me a headache. What's wrong, *cher*? Tell me."

"Marla...something happened...she's gone." I still couldn't quite believe it. No, I didn't want to. I wanted a barrier between me and that knowledge.

"Wait—what?"

I don't *know*! I wanted to scream.

"I don't know," I managed to say in a mostly normal decibel range. "Marla's gone. She was pulled away. The other ghosts can't find her."

When Marla vanished, the others were able to get in. They hovered near me now, not quite touching, but close as if they needed the proximity. I took some small shreds of comfort from that.

"You mean she was *exorcised*?" Solange asked, sounding pretty damn surprised.

Someone moaned. I realized it was me. Horrible sound.

I didn't want to deal with the truth. I wanted to believe that there was some way to get her back, that she wasn't completely out of reach.

Solange—maybe Solange could do something. She had that Voudon mojo, she had a spirit guide to assist her. Maybe she could find Marla and bring her back. Save her.

A tiny part of my brain pointed out that that was just wishful thinking, that I was denying the inevitable. I pointed a rocket launcher at that tiny part of my brain.

Denial, much?

"I can't deal with this," I said. Understatement.

"Hang on," Solange said. "I'll be there in half an hour. Sit tight. Lots of deep breaths. Ground if you can."

Any more deep breathing and I was going to pass out. I already felt lightheaded, except for my sinuses, which throbbed from the weeping and pressure.

I needed Tylenol, and I needed a drink.

Growing up, we had servants. Not a ton of them, but enough that when you needed something that wasn't within reach, you could make a request and that thing would appear. I missed that right now. Standing up and walking all the way to the parlor seemed about as doable as climbing Mt. Everest right now.

But sometimes you've just gotta suck it up.

I moved in kind of a stunned haze, but I was happy for it, because it allowed me to move. I closed the outside door to the solarium, which shouldn't have been open; collected a box of Kleenex from one of the bathrooms and sinus meds from my purse; poured whisky into a crystal glass; and counted myself impressive for having managed all of that.

Sometimes, it really is the little accomplishments that count.

I knocked back a shot of whisky while standing at the sideboard, poured more, and sat down in a brocade wing chair. Which was a good thing, because just then my phone rang, and I would've dropped that nice antique crystal glass. It was part of a set, you know.

I didn't recognize the number, so I let it go to voicemail while I forced myself to nurse the second whisky. Then I listened.

"Nikki? Hi, it's Donny. I'm sorry to be using your personal number—normally I wouldn't, but I was just a little concerned. As I was leaving the hotel, I nearly got plowed into by another car, and I just wanted to make sure everything was okay there, because that's where they seemed to be coming from. Um. Okay. Take care, bye."

Well, that was just…bizarre. I stared squinty-eyed at the phone. How had Donny gotten my number? And was he just trying to cover for himself? He could've snuck through the back while I was heading in the front….

"No, it was someone else," Sam said. This time I did shriek, but thankfully my glass was empty and the rug broke its fall.

"Sorry," he said. "Just wanted to say it wasn't Donny. He couldn't have gotten back there so fast. It was…already going on when you pulled up."

"Goddammit," I said. "Can you read my mind?"

"You were talking to yourself," he said. "I'm sorry. I didn't mean to startle you."

Deep breath. "That's okay," I said, retrieving the glass from the floor. I leaned my head back against the back of the chair. "S'not your fault. Did you see who came in, who did this?"

Sam sat on the edge of the loveseat, turning his hat in his hands. Watching it turn. He didn't want to look at me. I didn't blame him. I probably looked pretty disgusting. Red nose, swollen eyes, mascara everywhere. And let's not even talk about the drippy bits, 'kay?

"I'm sorry, no," he said, his voice low. "I...I wish I could have. We couldn't get into the room..."

I could hear it in his voice, no matter how hard he tried to be a 1940s stoic detective guy. Jesus. He was cracking up. This had ripped him up inside, too.

Marla may have been my friend, but there was one aspect of her life—afterlife—that I never shared. She'd been a ghost, and despite my minute and a half of clinical brain-deadedness a year ago, I was very much alive. (No *Sixth Sense* twists here, honest.)

Maybe Sam had been closer to her than I could ever have been. Maybe I could never call ghosts my friends, not really.

The world tilted, narrowed, and closed in until it was just me, in a chair, as alone as alone could be.

I was terrified.

FIFTEEN

FOR WHAT FELT LIKE FOREVER, I floated in that lonely darkness. Reaching out for Grandma Rosa, for Ned, for Marla, even for Eden, and greeted with no one.

Then I sensed Sam and Maggie and Janie and Curtis hovering somewhere nearby. I reached out blindly for a life-line, and although there was nobody I could physically touch, I knew they were there.

Marla, though, was still gone, forever out of my reach.

Somewhere in the hotel, a door slammed, and then I heard Solange calling my name.

I fought through the layers of muzziness and dizziness, and shouted that I was in the parlor. Thankfully it was loud enough for her to hear, because I didn't feel capable of getting up out of the chair, much less tracking her down in the depths of the hotel.

She found me, though, and swept me up in a big hug (I was able to stagger to my feet for that) that went on for as long as I needed it. I clung to her, breathing in a scent that reminded me of Grandma Rosa, of safety and security, and I bawled on her shoulder and she didn't even flinch.

When I finally released her, she scooped up my glass and replenished it, pouring herself a large whisky on the rocks in the process.

"Thank you for coming," I said. I curved my fingers around my glass, but didn't drink. I didn't need any more right now. I needed Solange to fix things.

"What happened, *cher*?" Solange asked, a warm, strong hand on my knee.

"Marla's gone," I said flatly. "I don't know how. I got here as it was happening, and couldn't get to her in time. She was in the solarium and nobody else could get in except me but it was too late. I brought you Krispy Kremes, but I think they got messed up. I'm sorry."

I started to cry again, dammit. Stupid effing donuts.

The other ghosts were gone, even Maggie, to wherever they go. They generally didn't stick around when Solange was here. In fact, other than Maggie, the rest of them generally made themselves scarce when other living people were around, except during the tours when they were performing their shtick.

Life, I think, sometimes makes them feel squicky.

"What do you mean, nobody could get in?" Solange asked.

I explained how the ghosts had somehow been blocked out of the solarium, although I'd had no problem getting in, flimsy lock notwithstanding.

"Have they experienced this kind of barrier before?" she asked.

Huh. I hadn't thought to ask. "I didn't get the chance to ask. It's never come up before now, though."

"And you believe Marla was taken against her will. That she didn't decide it was time to pass on."

I remembered the terror in Marla's eyes, the way her

fingers had scrabbled against the cushion, seeking purchase. I suspected the way she'd pleaded "Help me" would haunt my dreams.

I recalled Maggie's wail of anguish, and it all made me feel decidedly sick.

"It was like she was being tortured," I whispered. "So no, it wasn't by choice. Not even remotely."

"Nikki." Solange took my hands in hers. Her fingers were cool, and she had a way of holding your hands as if she were doing a reading on you, even if she wasn't looking at your palms or cards or anything. I shivered. I didn't feel up to having anybody, not even my most trusted friend, take a psychic gallivant around inside me.

Shields up, Captain. I felt guilty for it, but, well, tough.

"I know this has been awful for you," Solange said, her voice low and comforting. "I imagine it's akin to how I felt when Paul…"

God, I was an *idiot*.

Paul had been Solange's fiancé, back when she lived in Louisiana. They'd been mugged one night, walking home from a dinner and show. Paul had scuffled with the mugger and been shot. She'd watched him die.

Although she's tried, Solange has never been able to contact him. It's her real regret, and I've wished there were something I could do. To be able to tell somone one last time that you love them…

"I'm sorry," I said. My voice sounded very small. She didn't want to root around inside of me. Of course she didn't. God, I'm paranoid.

"No, I'm so, so sorry for what you're going through," she said. "You know I want to help you in any way I can." She hesitated, then asked, "Would you mind if I checked out the solarium? Maybe I can pick something up, a clue that would tell us who did this terrible thing."

"No, that's a good idea," I said. "I'll come with you." I put down my glass and started to stand.

"No, *cher*, you stay here and rest," she said, her hands now on my shoulders. "I'll take care of it. You're in no shape."

She had a good point. I was, no two ways about it, a royal mess.

But I couldn't just sit here. I couldn't do nothing. In fact, sitting here would send me back into the horrible nothing.

For Marla, I had to get up. For Marla, and for me.

"Coming with you," I said. "I need to."

Solange looked at me hard. "Okay," she said finally. "Okay."

It wasn't until we were in the solarium that I noticed Solange was carrying a large canvas tote bag with Star Dust's logo on it. It should have been hard to miss, but hey, I was distracted.

My stomach clenched when we walked in. I felt ice-water-doused sober and entirely sick again. The full moon glowed through the glass ceiling panels, the plants bathed silver, the familiar furniture and smell of dirt, all seemed unfair somehow. It shouldn't look normal, feel comfortable and welcoming.

"Did you see her in here?" Solange asked.

I pointed. "She was on that bench, holding on to it as if it would ground her and keep her here."

"Mm hm." Solange put her bag on the wicker table next to the bench and started pulling things out of it: a sage smudge tied with red yarn; a small, etched-brass bell; a stoppered, unfinished ceramic jar; an ancient-looking green glass bottle.

I stepped forwards to examine the tools more closely, but she waved me back.

"I'm sorry, *cher*," she said. "But your emotions are spewin' all over the place. I can't focus on anything if your energy is interfering."

"But I want to help." Marla was my friend, dammit.

She put her hands on my shoulders. "I know," she said. "But you're too messed up right now. It's not your fault—it's perfectly natural for you to be so upset right now. But in this state, you don't have the focus or control we need."

I knew she was right, but I didn't like it one bit. I stomped out of the room, grabbed a chair from the back parlor, and sat just inside the glass doors so I could watch her without, hopefully, letting my uncontrolled grief mess up her magical investigation.

So what if I was being pissy? Marla was my friend, and I was relegated to the audience like an understudy who'd never quite make the cut.

"Please turn off the lights. I'm going to contact my guide and try to get a picture of what happened here," Solange said, raising her voice slightly so I could hear her from my vantage point.

I did what she asked.

Having already removed her spikey sandals, she stood barefoot for a moment on the flagstones, arms at her sides with the palms facing forwards, her eyes closed. Grounding and centering, she called it. Opening herself to the energies of the earth and sky, wind and water and fire.

I felt a chill, and looked up to see the other ghosts crowded around me, also watching. Janie, Curtis, and Sam ringed behind me, Maggie at my side. Comforting, even without a touch.

"What's she doing?" Curtis asked.

"She's trying to figure out what happened to Marla," I said. "Maybe *see* who did it."

Solange glanced over at the sound of my voice. She didn't quite frown, but I got the distinct impression that she disapproved, that my words, not even directed at her, were enough to distract her and mess things up. Yes, she's able to send that without a real facial impression. She's that good.

"Sorry," I mouthed, and she smiled a little and went back to what she was doing.

"Hmph," Janie said. For some reason, Janie's never liked Solange. She's never said why, and I've just chalked it up to female rivalry, one of those times when two woman just react to each other like the opposite of magnets, whatever that's called. Repelling each other without knowing why.

Solange has never said much about Janie, but she doesn't seem to have much of a rapport with any of my ghosts. Well, maybe that's overthinking. Curtis seems to like Solange, and Marla always liked everybody....

My throat closed. I couldn't go fetal in a straight chair, but I still managed to hunch over pretty far, protecting my stomach and the pain there.

Solange unstoppered the ceramic jar and sprinkled salt in a wide circle around the wicker bench. The circumference included into some of the plants, and I wondered how the salt would affect them. I wisely didn't ask Janie what she thought.

Okay, I knew a salt circle was sort of a way to keep spirits in or out. I didn't quite get why it was needed here, but truthfully, I'm not up on all the ritual stuff. That's Solange's forte. Me, I just hang out with ghosts.

She followed up the salt with splashes of liquid from the bottle, then lit the bundle of sage. The smoke wafted over to me, a comforting warm scent, so familiar. Right now, it was making me sleepy...or maybe that was the whisky and the fact that my sinuses were still all blocked to hell.

Plus, although I desperately wanted to know who had done this to Marla, I had to admit that *watching* someone else go through the motions was boring as hell.

Finally Solange walked the circle while ringing the brass bell and chanting in a low, sonorous voice. I couldn't make out the words, but a slow chill trailed its fingers down my back.

Then she sat on the bench, and I winced, because it was almost like Marla was still there, even though she wasn't.

It's a problem you get when you spend time with ghosts. Sometimes you hesitate before you sit in a chair, because you're not entirely sure whether someone's already sitting there or not.

You have to be extra-careful about not stopping and staring at chairs before you sit if someone else is around. It's hard to explain away.

We waited, the only illumination from the parlor behind me, spilling onto the flagstones. I didn't know what to expect. A sudden flash? A vision? Or was I too far outside the circle.

I dabbed my nose with a crumpled piece of Kleenex I still had in my hand. I really needed to blow, but I was afraid the noise would mess things up.

"Are you picking anything up?" I whispered to Janie, who was closest to me.

She shook her head. Damn.

Finally Solange roused herself. She picked up the still-smoldering sage bundle and walked counter-clockwise, to open the circle or whatever. Then she crushed it out in the dirt, scuffed some of the salt so the ring was broken, and came over to me and crouched in front of my chair like I was a little kid and she was getting down to my level. The ghosts faded away, except for Maggie, who moved behind me.

"There were definitely some strong forces at work here," she said. "Surprisingly strong."

"But who was it?" I asked. "Or *what*?"

She shook her head. "I'm...I'm not sure yet. I need to process, meditate on what I've been given."

"But how do I stop whomever it is from doing it again? I don't want this evil thing fucking with my friends!" I realized my hands were shaking from my helpless rage.

She hugged me as best she could, but it was hard to relax into it. "*Cher*, give me some time to figure it out. We could be reading this all wrong. We don't really know what keeps them here or what calls them to the other side. Maybe the call—"

"It's not like that," I insisted, frustrated and angry and grieving and probably the tiniest bit irrational. "They've told me they have the choice, that it's not a compulsion or a force they can't control. Somebody or some*thing* caused this to happen."

"Just because it's a choice doesn't mean it's the right one," Solange said. "People make bad decisions every day."

I reared back. "What are you saying?"

"I'm not saying *anything* yet," Solange said. "I still need to process it all. But right now, you go get shoes on and wash your face and fix your hair, because I'm taking you out to eat. You look like you haven't eaten in a week."

"I had canapés," I said, but admittedly the hors d'oeuvres—the entire party—felt like a lifetime time ago. Oh, and the donut. "Can't we just order a pizza or something?" The idea of getting up and tidying myself and finding shoes seemed interminably difficult and tiring. Plus I felt a flutter of panic at the idea of leaving the hotel and leaving my friends vulnerable.

Not that I knew what I could do to protect them if I *was* here. But not being here seemed worse, like I'd be abandoning them.

"There's nothing you can do here right now," Solange said as if reading my mind. "And getting out will do you a world of good." She stood and tugged at me. I rose reluctantly, my legs unsteady and weak.

But my ghostly companions stuck close. I felt like I was standing in front of an air conditioner that wasn't blowing. (That didn't really make sense, which showed my mental state right now.) As much as I loved Solange, these guys needed me more.

They were grieving, too.

We'd find comfort together.

"No," I said again. "Really, I'm okay. Not great, but okay. I want to take a shower and a sleeping pill and crash."

She looked at me for a long moment, lips pursed, and then sighed. "If you're sure you'll be fine alone."

"I'm not alone," I said, gesturing.

"Of course you're not," she said quickly. "Sorry. All right. Come by the shop tomorrow—I'll put together a tisane to help you rest, help you sleep. And we still have a date to watch the AAMies."

"You betcha." I tried to summon up enough emotion to care about some award show.

I walked her to the gate at the end of the front courtyard.

She hit the remote to unlock her car. "You're sure you don't want to come?"

"Nah," I said. "Go home. Be safe. And thank you."

In the glow of the streetlamp, I saw her smile. "Anything for you, *cher*."

I sighed. It didn't make me feel much better.

SIXTEEN

I NEVER MADE IT UPSTAIRS. I woke up on a fainting couch in the lobby at about five a.m., thinking it must have been a hell of a party. The glass on the floor next to me held a few drops of whisky, and I was *pretty* sure I hadn't had more than one glass.

I remembered talking to Janie for a little while, asking how she was holding up, and waking up once to tell Curtis that I really didn't need The Cure's "Lullaby" over and over to help me sleep, but that was about it.

Maggie was sitting in the wing chair closest to the couch, arms wrapped around her knees, looking miserable. Although I was relieved to see her, it took me several tries to voice the question I feared the answer to.

"Is everybody still here?"

She nodded. I breathed out.

I didn't have a headache, for which I was deeply grateful, but I was muzzy and bleary-eyed and someone had put little fuzzy socks on my teeth.

What I did have was a fresh wave of stomach-clenching

misery as last night's memories hit me harder than the last King Arthur movie bombed.

What I also had, when I fumbled for my phone and squinted at it, was a text.

"Prty 2day bch hse noon. See U thr. Chris."

I...what?

I shook my phone, shook my head. Maybe I was hallucinating. Maybe I wasn't awake yet. No, my bladder was telling me I was awake. I looked at my phone again, and the text was still there.

The message was clearly from my friend Chris Yeates, whom I hadn't talked to since...well, other than when I'd interrupted her and Evan at the movie premiere, I think I've talked to her once after I got out of rehab. Maybe twice. She invited me to one or two things, I declined because I was so not in the right space, end of story.

Well, not completely. I did find a few veiled, vague comments in her Snapchat feed before I canceled my Snapchat account entirely. (Because I had nobody to talk to on it anymore. That may be the saddest moment of my life after losing Grandma Rosa and now Marla.)

She and Eden and I had been the Terrific Triad, the Three Musketeerettes, BFFs and all that. They'd both dropped me like a Kardashian first husband.

So why was she inviting me to a party at her beach house tonight?

Maybe it was a last-ditch effort to see if I'd actually show.

I stood, shoved my phone in my pocket, hit the bathroom, dragged myself to the kitchen, my steps slow. The big white box of Krispy Kremes was still on the floor. I automatically picked it up and set it on the stainless steel island.

The coffee maker was on. "Thank you, Janie," I said to

136 DAYLE A. DERMATIS

empty air. I wasn't hung over, but I should probably eat. I poured coffee, selected a smashed donut, and stared at both.

Parties like this didn't require an RSVP, so I'd have all morning to think about it. I was pretty sure I'd need it.

I WENT BACK and forth about the party all morning. While I showered, standing so the hot water hit my face for as long as I could stand it, draining my sinuses. While I coordinated the next few tour requests, paid bills, placed an order for tea sandwiches. While I paced through the ground floor of the hotel, avoiding the solarium.

On one hand, I'd pretty much been written out of everyone's lives, and I'd mostly made peace with that. I wasn't a party girl anymore.

On the other hand, the idea of a mindless, loud party where nobody talked about anything more important than the latest fashions or who was cheating on whom with whom sounded like exactly what I needed. Distraction.

On one hand, Evan's and Chris's reactions to me at the premiere made me think this was some kind of sick setup.

On the other hand, maybe I needed more living friends, and surely not everyone hated me. In that crowd, alliances changed all the time.

I went back and forth, back and forth, trying not to think about Marla.

But I had to think about Marla. And Aaron, and Thomas and Bertha. And Tabitha and Sam, and Otter.

When my phone buzzed to let me know I had an email, my first thought was that it was Chris to tell me that the invitation was a mistake.

I couldn't have been more wrong.

Hi, this is Rudy Schwabach from Ominous Spiritus. Sorry to bother you, but is everything okay? I detected some seriously weird readings at your place last night. Did something happen?

Also, I'm sorry I broke into your place the other night. That was stupid. I hope you don't report it to the police.

Rudy

Rudy? Detected seriously weird readings at my place last night?

Understatement of the year when it came to the readings. But what did he mean, he detected them? Detected them how? With what?

Had he planted detecting devices in my Ballington?

I might have to turn *him* into a ghost.

Then again...maybe his detecting devices had turned up something useful—maybe he had recorded who had taken Marla. I felt a glimmer of hope. Solange was working on her end, but Rudy's technobabble stuff could give another part of the picture.

No doubt scaring the hell out of him again, I emailed him back immediately.

THE STAR DUST front door opened silently as usual, and I was greeted with some kind of harp music. In the short time since I'd been here, the place had exploded with suns. Candle holders, knickknacks, strands of beads and lights, jewelry, plus sunflowers and candles shading from yellow to red. It was nearly the Summer Solstice, the longest day and shortest night of the year.

A few weeks ago it had been Chinese dragon kites, hanging from the ceiling by invisible lines, for the Dragon Boat Festival, or Duanwu Festival, Solange had told me. I couldn't keep track of all of them: Celtic, Nordic, Mayan, whatever. Bridget must have to decorate every damn day of the year for something.

"Hi, Nikki," Bridget said when I approached the glass counter.

"Hey."

"Solange isn't here, I'm afraid." Her red curls were pulled back and threaded through with silver and green ivy leaves, framing her sharp-cheekboned face. Matching earrings dangled from her lobes, and her eyeliner was green, making her blue eyes look even more fierce.

"D'you know when she'll be back?" I asked.

She shook her head. "She's running some errands for the store. She left something for you, though." She reached under the counter, but seemed to hesitate before she pulled out a small Star Dust bag with its purple-and-gold logo and handed it to me.

Curious myself, I peered into the bag and pulled out a cobalt-blue glass jar. I shook it, but whatever was inside was pretty light.

"There's a note," Bridget said. I thought I heard something in her voice; a little tightness, maybe. Nah, I was probably imagining things—unless she was mad at Solange for giving me a present or something.

I opened the envelope and unfolded the handmade paper imbedded with bits of flower petals. In Solange's looping handwriting, it said,

Cher: Here's a tisane for you. Take it at night with a dollop of organic clover honey; it'll help you sleep. It aids in dreaming, and you know REM time is vital to restful sleep.

Plus, maybe in your dreams you'll catch something you missed before about what happened to poor Marla. I'm sorry I'm taking so long with my part of the research. Much love, Solange.

I put the note and jar back in the bag, and raised the bag as if I was making a toast. "Thanks, Bridget," I said. "'preciate it."

"Nikki..."

Okay, now I was sure I was hearing something in her voice.

She'd schooled her face so I couldn't read her expression. At another time I might have spent a moment envying her smooth, pale complexion (do the Irish not *have* pores?), but now I was mostly just trying to figure out what the hell was going on with her.

"Be careful," she said finally. "I don't know what-all Solange put in that tisane, but some ingredients can react funny with different people."

"Oh, don't worry," I said breezily. "I've had Solange's teas before. She knows my allergies and stuff."

Bridget was probably just uncomfortable with Solange taking the time out of her busy day to create the mixture for me.

The suns beamed at me as I left, exiting into the bright afternoon Venice sunlight. A few minutes later, I was in my car and heading to the party in Malibu.

For better or worse.

SEVENTEEN

I'D DECIDED to go to Chris's party.

It seemed like it should have been a simple decision, but it wasn't. Not by a long, long shot.

I felt like I had after my grandmother's funeral: adrift and in need of distraction, in need of the familiar. I also felt helpless—Rudy couldn't meet me until tomorrow, Tabitha and Marilyn didn't have updates, and I didn't have any other resources to throttle until information fell out. The rest of the ghosts in the hotel were lying low; if I'd thought I should throw a wake, I would, but it felt weird somehow.

There's nothing I hate worse than being alone with my own thoughts when I feel like this.

So I decided, fuck it, I'm going to the party. If it sucks, I can leave.

I'd thrown on a retro pink sundress with black polka dots that I thought looked updated fifties and Curtis thought looked clearly eighties, an argument neither of us was ever going to give in on. Right now, though, I didn't care.

Is this what it's like when you get old? You lose someone, and all of a sudden everyone else in your life is more precious, to the point where even the most annoying traits in someone become endearing?

Because it kind of bites. I didn't want to develop a sudden fondness for Curtis's idiosyncrasies any more than I wanted to wax rhapsodic over Marla's stoned flakiness, which used to drive me nuts.

But if I didn't, how would I remember her? I bit my lip to keep it from quivering. She hadn't driven me *that* nuts. Neither did Curtis, nor Sam and Janie or anyone else.

Jaysus, I didn't want to be thinking about this. The party was sounding better and better, if only because I didn't have my board to go surfing. No. Seriously. I wanted to be around people, and have a good time, and laugh and dance and party.

That's not too much to ask, is it?

I pulled up to the gatehouse outside the Malibu estate and keyed in the code. I'd been afraid it had been changed since the last time I was here, but thankfully no. The wrought iron gate slid sideways and I eased through.

There were already a fair number of cars there. I parked next to an M&M-yellow Hummer. Who in their right mind buys a Hummer in M&M yellow? It looked ridiculous. And whoever drove it parked as if a large, bright-yellow whale had died and flopped down haphazardly, with no relation to the other cars around it.

The party was in full swing, with loud laugher, louder conversations, and even louder music. Like most houses with ocean view and access, the house wasn't much to look at from the front. The back, though, was a wall of floor-to-ceiling windows to maximize the view. Through the windows I could see people on the porch dancing.

There was a sunken seating area in the middle of the

main room, and Eden and Chris were standing at the edge of it. Eden had a martini in one hand and a cigarette in the other. Her blond hair was a bit shorter, wavier, with bangs. Chris had something that was probably heavily laced with vodka, unless her tastes had changed in the last year. She had her blond hair in a messy braid over one shoulder. (Yes, we were all blonds. Celebrity followers prefer them, don't you know.)

For a moment I had a weird sense of...something. Déjà vu, maybe. The world tilted and blurred, images juxtaposing over this one. A vision of the last party, the one where I'd stumbled in wanting something to numb the pain, and I'd gotten it in spades.

I shook my head to clear it. I wouldn't make the same mistake again, so there was nothing to worry about. The fact that it all seemed familiar was a *good* thing, a comfortable feeling.

That and the fact that there were no ghosts here. Maggie had chosen to stay in the car. I loved my other-worldly friends, but today, just for a little while, I needed to pretend everything was normal. That the world was normal.

That *I* was normal.

Eden and Chris were laughing when I walked up to them. "Hey guys!" I said.

Their laughter stopped abruptly, as if they'd just heard La Perla had stopped making thongs. They both gave near-identical blinks of surprise.

"Nikki!" Chris said. "What are you—I...didn't expect to see you here. How did you hear about the party?"

At the same time, I thought I heard Eden say, "Dammit, did Ned...?"

What did Ned have to do with it? "Uh, you texted me,

beeyatch," I said lightly to Chris, using our old term of endearment.

Eden's head whipped around so she could glare at Chris with a look reserved for a TMZ reporter. Chris blinked again. "I did?"

"Early this morning." I reached into my purse. "Want to see?"

"No, no, that's okay," Chris said. "I totally forgot. I've been so busy since I started my fashion line of purses you can carry your fish around in. Tiny dogs are so last decade. Maybe you've seen them? Anyway, it's great to see you!"

She hugged me in that half-hug way someone does when they don't want to spill their drink. Eden gave me a similar hug.

"I have to hit the bathroom," Eden said, waggling her martini glass. "S'cuze."

Chris excused herself to talk to someone who'd just come in, telling me to get myself a drink.

Buoyed up by the positive reception from them, I got a lemon drop from the bar and wandered around saying hello to people, many of whom looked surprised and then hugged me, asking me how I was. At least in this crowd, nobody thought I'd been dead, which was a nice change.

And nobody *was* dead.

"Nikki!"

I turned to find the source of the delighted squeal, and found myself in a hug that actually caused me to spill *my* drink right down my pretty vintage dress.

Big problem: I couldn't remember who she was.

I wracked my brains, and for once my mother's training served me well. Since I was a kid, she'd hammered in to me the concept that remembering people was crucial. She'd quiz me at parties, even. Names first, then relationships

("And who is she married to? Can you point him out?") and then trivia (how many kids, what movies they'd produced, yadda yadda).

"Asia!" I said. "It's been for*ev*er."

I'd met her only a few times before I'd dropped out of the party circuit, because she'd been a hanger-on, trying to get into the circle and be famous. Apparently it had worked.

Asia McBride, that was it. A mix of Asian and Scottish ancestry that had resulted in an extremely cute young thing, glossy black hair and exotic eyes paired with a smattering of freckles and more curves than you'd expect. A younger, bubblier Lucy Liu, with a strong hint of Marilyn, actually.

She'd just started on some reality show, *Mission Hills* or *Back to the Beach* or one of those, and it had taken off. Or she'd taken off. Honestly, I never have time to watch TV much anymore, and what's real about reality shows?

It was all coming back to me. She was nice enough, as I recalled, but way too...enthusiastic. Like a puppy that wags its tail so hard, its ass nearly falls off.

Maybe Asia's ass shaking was why she was moving up the ladder. I really don't know. Not my place to judge.

"It *so* good to see you!" Asia said. "I've been wondering how you'd been, but nobody seemed to have your number anymore. I love your hair, by the way. And that dress you wore to the premiere! I'd kill for your figure, I really would. Oh, and this dress is really cool. Who is it?"

"It's vintage," I said, kind of pleased. "Thanks. How have you been?" I asked, because that's what I'd been taught to do: they say something nice, you express interest in them, and so on. "How's the show going?"

"Oh, it's fabulous," she said, and she was off. I confess I kind of tuned her out as I scanned the crowd for Chris or

Eden. If Asia paused for breath, I'd ask her if she'd seen them.

She didn't. Pause for breath, that is.

Finally I said I had to clean off my dress, and she nodded in understanding, although she kept talking for a good twenty seconds longer before her head whipped around and she said, "Is that Lamar Tinibu?" And then she was off.

I looked. It wasn't Lamar.

Both of the bathrooms on this floor were occupied, so I sought out the one upstairs. It was off one of the opulent bedrooms, with another deck overlooking the ocean. The bathroom itself had a tub you could do laps in. I'm pretty sure someone got drunk enough at a previous party to try.

There was nobody in the bedroom, but I heard voices on the deck. I would've left, but I heard my name.

"I can't believe you invited Nikki!" It was Eden, and she was spitting mad. "Jesus, Chris! What were you thinking?"

"Calm the fuck down," Chris said, not sounding much happier. "I couldn't find my phone, so I used another one. I sent a bulk message about the party; I didn't know she was on the old list."

"She's an embarrassment," Eden said.

My head whipped back as if she'd physically slapped me. My stomach hitched, and I tasted lemon-tinged bile. Ew.

"Do you think *I* want her here?" Chris demanded. "Everyone's looking at me as if I'm the freak."

"Tell them you felt sorry for her or something," Eden said. "Just make sure you don't 'accidentally' invite her again. She's yesterday's news. Besides, what if she finds out about me and—"

Her and who? My ears perked up. Someone she didn't

want me to know about. Evan? Jesse? Marco Valeri behind Jennifer Bianchi's back? (A highly unwise idea. Jennifer could kick Eden's ass from here to next Tuesday without breaking a sweat. *And* still get all her kids to school on time.)

But a phone rang right then, and Eden didn't finish her damn sentence and put me out of my curiosity.

"Hey baby," she cooed into the phone (I assumed, since I couldn't see her). "I was just thinking about you. It's been sooooo long since this morning.... You're at the front gate? I'll be right down..."

"Well, I guess she's going to find out soon enough," Chris commented.

"Fuck her," Eden said. "Hand me that straw."

Idiots. Never do coke on an open balcony—one random balmy sea breeze and *poof*.

Not to mention the chance of a pap with a long lens and a good eye.

"Hey, maybe we should offer some to Nikki," Chris said.

Eden laughed. It wasn't pretty. "Seriously. Then maybe she'd go away again."

Ow. *Ow.* If she'd kicked me in the stomach, it wouldn't have hurt more. Fuck me? Fuck *her*. Fuck *both* of them.

But I had no interest in a confrontation. No chick fights for me, thanks.

I was out of here.

I did duck into another bathroom to dab at the lemon drop stain on my vintage dress in the hopes that it wouldn't set, and to take a couple of deep breaths that didn't help at all. Fuck yoga, too.

I headed down the stairs, and as I neared the bottom, I saw Eden fly through the foyer towards the front door squealing "You're here!" Crap, they'd gotten down ahead of me. Well, I'd wait until she and the newcomer crossed the foyer and went deeper into the house.

But they didn't. Nobody passed by the foot of the stairs. Maybe Eden had gone outside with the newcomer?

I went to the last step and peered around the corner. Chris was hugging Evan Frohman. Eden had launched herself into another guy's arms, her legs wrapped around his waist, and they were kissing in a way that made me wonder if he was just going to do her up against the wall any minute now.

Then he raised his head, smiling down at her, and my jaw literally dropped. For the second time in less than half an hour, I felt like someone had planted a steel-toed boot in my gut.

Ned.

My brother was dating Eden Everly, knowing my past with her.

Okay, Ned was mad at me, but this just felt like *betrayal*.

You know what? Screw 'em. All of them. Ned, Eden, Chris, everyone. Yes, it hurt like hell, but I'd been through worse. I'd nearly died. I'd had one of my best friends ripped away from me only yesterday. This kind of petty shit was nothing.

They were lapping at each other again, I turned away from the front door, pushed my way through the crowd in the living room.

And that's when things went *really* bad.

EIGHTEEN

I FELT like a salmon swimming upstream. The word had gotten out that Evan, star of *Day Into Knight*, which had had a massive box office over the weekend, had arrived. Everyone was surging towards the front of the house, and my goal was to get out the back.

Nobody paid one whit of attention to me. I could've been a ghost myself.

The only person who hadn't joined the throng was Asia. She was sitting on the edge of the hot tub on the back patio, her feet in the water. She was on her cell phone, yelling at someone. As I came outside, she shouted, "Fine, then you're fired!" and flung the phone on the redwood slats of the patio.

"Are all agents completely useless?" she asked when she saw me.

"Probably," I said. Then, not wanting to get stuck in a conversation with her, I added, "Did you hear Evan Frohman just arrived?"

Her head whipped around. "Really?"

I didn't stay for more. I headed off the deck into the

sand towards the side of the house. I'd sneak through between the houses, get in my car, and get the hell out of here forever.

But just as I rounded the corner, I heard a splash, and I had to glance back.

Asia had fallen into the hot tub.

I took a few steps back, then froze as I saw crimson spreading through the water like—well, pick your horror movie. Start with *Jaws*, it's a classic. My hands flew to my mouth.

Okay, I had to pull her out of the water and call 911. Okay, I could do that.

I ran back to the hot tub and knelt beside it, but then I saw something else. Something nobody else would be able to see.

A fine blue mist rising from Asia's unmoving form. It didn't really coalesce, didn't really take full shape, but I knew what it was. Her soul (or essence or whatever) leaving her body. Moving on to the next plane.

Asia was beyond help.

Despite the fact that I hang out with dead people all the time, I'd never actually seen a dead body until now. I don't mean like someone in a funeral home, laid out and prettified. I mean still warm.

Worse, I'd been talking to Asia just seconds ago. I was having a hard time comprehending that she just *wasn't* anymore, almost more than I had with Marla. It made no sense.

Was this what being in shock felt like?

I swallowed back the bile that rose in my throat. Now I had to get out of here before anyone spotted me near Asia's body. I hadn't done anything, and my father had very, very good lawyers who'd make sure everything would be okay, but the publicity...oh Jaysus, the publicity. Not after my whole ODing-and-dying thing. Not when Daddy's movie had just become a hit.

I scrambled to my feet and went back the way I'd been going. Problem was, I couldn't stop myself from glancing back again when I hit the corner of the house.

The blue mist had stopped rising to the heavens. Had stopped being a blue mist. Asia McBride's ghost was going back into the party, heaven help them.

And heaven help me, but I had to go look.

It was all I could do not to fall into little pieces.

She was stumbling her way through the crowd, although nobody could actually feel her and she was filtering in and out. Each person she touched jumped back, squicked out by the sensation of icy slime.

From here I couldn't hear anything, but I could see her lips moving as she waved her hands in front of people's faces, trying to get their attention. Her movements were getting bigger and crazier, and she was crying, begging.

Sometimes, even if you have choices, it doesn't feel like you any—other than the obvious right one.

I waded into the milling mass of half-drunk, half-drugged, oblivious people, and grabbed Asia by the arm. My hand shivered towards numbness, but I gritted my teeth and held on.

"Come with me," I hissed. She turned wild eyes on me, her expression making it clear she was halfway to hysteria and her speed in that direction was rapidly increasing. "Asia!" I said, just as quietly but with as much urgency as I could force into my voice.

If anyone heard me talking to nothing, my reputation as being more batshit insane than Britney Spears would be solidified forever. I wouldn't even have to shave my head or barricade myself in the bathroom with my kids or anything.

"Nikki?" she whimpered. "Nikki, what's going on? Why won't they talk to me?"

"I'll explain. Follow me." I tugged at her arm, and she followed obediently, like a puppy, clinging to my belt like a lifeline.

I dragged her upstairs to the opulent bedroom and locked the door behind us. I sat her down on the edge of the bed and dragged the vanity stool over so I could sit facing her.

She was dry, at least. Maybe she didn't remember falling into the hot tub. It would suck wandering around dripping like Moaning Myrtle for the rest of your undead life.

"Asia," I said, and then stopped. Holy expiration, Batman, how do you tell someone they've kicked the bucket? My only experience had been with ghosts who'd been dead for a while and had warmed to the idea. Well, maybe not "warmed," given their chill, but the point was that all the ghosts I knew had come to terms with their own lack of mortality well before I'd come on the scene.

I had no expertise in this area. Not a freaking clue.

What would Dr. Phil do? Or was this a Dr. Oz issue?

I had no idea. I decided to go for the simplest approach, or, at least, the most direct.

"Asia," I said. "I have some really bad news."

"I know," she said sadly.

"You do?" When had she figured it out?

She nodded. "That wasn't Lamar Tinibu downstairs earlier."

I resisted the urge to clutch at my hair and scream through gritted teeth. Might unnerve her.

"That's not what I'm talking about," I said. "It's worse, I'm afraid. I need you to really listen to me, okay, and try not to freak out."

She nodded again, her eyes wide. She looked like she totally trusted me, and I felt like shit for having to be the one to give her the news.

"Um. You're dead."

"What?" Her brow furrowed. Statement has no meaning. Does not compute.

"Not 'dead' like 'in trouble'," I clarified. "*Dead* dead. You fell into the hot tub and hit your head. Look, you're up here, but your body's down there, okay?"

She looked down at herself. Her skirt was rumpled, but otherwise she seemed intact.

"Are you sure?" she asked dubiously. "I don't *feel* dead... I don't think. I feel funny, but you said I hit my head?"

I got up and went out to the balcony and peered over. I had a clear view of the redwood patio extending out below. The rays of the sun sinking over the ocean illuminated the scene.

I swallowed hard and motioned her over to me.

Her wail of horror was so loud and piercing that I worried somebody might actually hear. I stepped back in surprise, and she lunged for me, grabbing my forearm with both hands as if she thought I was leaving her forever. It felt as though I'd immersed my arm in a mountain stream before all the winter ice had melted away.

If a bone-frosting mountain stream was combined with primordial goo, that is.

I'd have to explain the no-touching rule to her very soon.

I managed to get back into the room and get her seated again so I could peel her off of me.

"So...I'm a ghost?" she asked.

I nodded.

"What does that mean?"

"I'm not completely sure," I said. "Look, I know some other ghosts—let me take you to them and they can explain things better."

She shrank back. "Noooo, ghosts are scary!"

Ye gods. "They're no different than you, hon," I pointed out. "You're dead; they're dead. They're actually pretty nice."

"You won't leave me?" she asked. She didn't quite whimper again, but I sensed she still teetered on the edge of a nervous breakdown.

I hadn't really wanted to hang out with Asia while she was alive, but I felt like I had some sort of responsibility here, given that I was the only person I knew who could actually see and interact with her.

The least I could do was take her to the Ballington, let Janie take her under her wing, and when Asia was cool with her new state of being, she'd wander off to do whatever it is she wanted to do that was keeping her here. Maybe she'd haunt her own reality show and screw up the cameras. That would be kind of funny.

"Nope, I won't," I said. "To that end, let's get the hell out of here."

I was at the bedroom door when I realized that wasn't going to be as easy as it sounded. "Damn," I said.

"What's wrong?" she asked.

"I don't want to go down where people will see me. They'll remember I was here, and tell the cops when they arrive, and the cops will want to interview everyone who was here. They do that sort of thing when there's a dead body."

"Somebody *died*?!" Asia put her hand to her mouth.

I gave her A Look, and she had the good graces to look abashed. She might've blushed if she had the blood to do that with.

"Oh God," she said. "This is so weird. I don't *feel* dead. Should I feel dead? What's dead supposed to feel like?"

I had no idea. I can tell ghosts from real people by a vague Spidey-sense, but I had no idea what the world was like from their perspective. Maybe once she started filtering through walls, she'd get comfortable with her new state. Hopefully my friends could help her with that.

I chewed my lip, ruining my lipstick, as I thought about what to do.

"What are you waiting for?" Asia asked. "Let's go."

She was standing at the French doors to the balcony. Confused, I walked over to her, and turned my gaze to where she pointed.

The balcony was a deck that had stairs leading down to the sand.

Well, didn't I feel like an idiot.

NINETEEN

I HAD Maggie and Asia walk in front of and behind the car as I drove up to the security gate, then through it, in the hopes their presence would blur my license plates in any security camera feeds. Maybe I watch too many crime shows, but it pays to be safe, right?

Thankfully there were no paparazzi outside. After the no-touching rule, I'd have to break the new to Asia that photo ops were a thing of the past for her. If she wasn't already dead, she'd probably fling herself off a cliff at that news.

THE NEXT DAY, I met Rudy Schwabach at a random Baja Fresh near-ish to the hotel. I wore my usual floppy hat and sunglasses, but now with *two* ghosts tagging along with me, I was extra-safe from the paps. But I still wasn't in the mood for random autograph hounds or weirdos.

Then again, look at me. If avoiding weirdos was my goal, I was failing miserably.

See, I'd already discovered that I'd made a minor splash just by appearing at the party. Near the end of a blog post about Asia's death (which wasn't officially determined, but was expected to be ruled accidental head injury), there was a picture of me, lemon drop martini glass in hand, from Chris's beach house. The fact that it was kind of grainy made me think it had been taken with a camera phone, because I hadn't seen any cameras around that day—at least, none obviously pointed at me.

The caption read, "Back to her partying ways?" Oh please.

The blog went on, "It's been a while since we've seen Nikki Ashburne on the party circuit. What's the reason for her return? Boredom? Misses the limelight? The bottom line is, if she's going to show up more often, we just hope she makes some better choices about her hair."

I had self-consciously raised a hand to my head before I realized what I was doing. My hair was just fine, dammit.

Anyway, just in case my presence had caused an upsurge of interest in me, I wanted to be especially careful for a while.

The place looked like every other Baja Fresh: airy and white inside, with a black-and-white checked floor, the only color the green and red logo on the wall. Generic poppy Mexican music playing; whenever I hear it anywhere else, I suddenly develop a wild craving for Baja Fresh. Tall two-person bistro tables with stools and normal four-person tables with chairs. Rudy had headed for a bistro table, but I'd steered him to a regular one.

After all, it would be rude to leave my other friends standing, right?

Asia plopped down in her chair, put her elbow on the table and her chin on her hand, and stared at Rudy in a way that made me a little uncomfortable. I couldn't exactly ask her what was up, not in front of Rudy. Not yet.

I couldn't even smack her to make her stop. Argh.

While we waited for our food, I went through my usual routine of gathering condiments from the Salsa Bar. Two little plastic tubs of pico de gallo with the brown medium-heat salsa poured over the little tomato and onion and cilantro bits, for dipping the fresh salty tortilla chips in. Nummers. Two little tubs of sliced jalapeños. Two little tubs of lime slices from the drinks area—they're probably to drop in your soda, but I like to squeeze them on my burrito, okay? Lids for half of those, because I can never finish a whole burrito in one sitting.

Rudy had a cheese quesadilla. How unimaginative. When I reminded him I was buying, he got a side order of guacamole, at least.

They called our number, and Rudy got up before I did to grab the tray. I dug into my burrito. Rudy nibbled at his quesadilla, eyeing me all the while. I'd responded to his email about seriously weird readings at the hotel by saying I wanted to meet. I hadn't explained why, exactly. I'd just said we needed to talk.

As the cliché goes, "We need to talk" is something nobody wants to hear, ever.

I didn't know how to begin, so I just jumped right in. "I need your help with something, but first I need you to sign this nondisclosure agreement." I slid the papers over to him. Just two pages, fairly simple. He couldn't reveal anything he learned about me, my family, or the hotel.

"Are you serious?" he asked.

"This is Hollywood," I said. "There are some things we don't take chances with. You can have your attorney review it if you want to."

He wiped his hands on a paper napkin and read the pages carefully while I nibbled at my burrito. "Okay," he said, and scrawled at the bottom of the second page. I added my signature, and we both signed a second copy for him to keep.

"Second thing before we go on," I said. "What exactly did you mean by getting weird readings at the hotel the other night? How are you monitoring the hotel? If you left any recording devices in the hotel, you have to tell me. Right. Now. If I find out you've lied to me..."

He paled. Apparently I *am* that threatening. "No, no," he said hastily. "I didn't put anything in or around the hotel." He pushed his glasses up his nose and took a deep breath. "But sometimes I drive by, and from my car, I take readings. For paranormal activity *only*. I'm not spying on you. In fact, I try to do it when I think you're not there. If that guy with a camera isn't outside, sometimes that's a good indication."

Oh, Donny. I'd have to warn him his every move was under scrutiny.

"The other night, my EMF went bananas. Readings off the charts. But then you came home, and I stayed only a couple more minutes, I swear. Then it stopped, and I left right away. But I was concerned, which is why I emailed you."

He looked so earnest, I found it hard to believe he could be lying. He'd have to be a really good actor, and I just didn't think he was.

"Okay," I said. "So, do we have a deal? Will you help me?"

He squinted. "Not before I know what you want me to do, and what I get out of it."

"Oh, that's easy," I said. "They're kind of the same

thing. You get full access to the Ballington to search for ghosts. And I can assure you, they're real."

He blinked, and put down the triangle of quesadilla he'd been about to bite into. "How do I know you won't be faking them?" he asked.

I squeezed some lime on my burrito, carefully placed a slice of jalapeño, and took a bite. Was I really desperate enough to tell him the truth?

I remembered the terrified expression on Marla's face before she was ripped away. Yes, I was.

The place was almost empty; it was early afternoon, after the lunch rush had faded. No one close enough to hear my crazytalk.

I washed the mouthful of burrito down with Diet Pepsi. "You probably know that about a year ago, I was clinically dead for a couple of minutes. Well, when I came to, I could see ghosts. And I can show them to you."

I'd had a talk with everyone last night. It had taken a little while because Asia had to be brought up to speed on the whole ghosts-disappearing thing, and it freaked her out, and she wouldn't stop talking until I got a little mad at her. Janie comforted her, which helped. Janie was more of a mother figure than my own mother sometimes. Okay, most of the time.

All of them agreed to become visible or otherwise obvious to Rudy, because they'd loved Marla, too.

And because even if they didn't say it, they were scared.

Rudy put his hands on the table as if he wanted to stand up again. But he didn't. His fingers flexed, but he stayed put, curiosity and the need to believe outweighing his suspicions.

"You can see ghosts," he said dubiously.

I nodded. "Ever since I died and was revived."

He reached for his soda, took a long drink through the straw. "Okay," he said finally. "So you can see ghosts."

I nodded. "There are two here with us right now."

He reared back, dark eyes wide in a face that hadn't fully regained color yet.

"Why do you think I wanted a table with four chairs?" I pointed out. "I don't suppose you have an EMF-thingy in that bag at your feet."

His eyes rolled sideways, as if he were thinking. No doubt he was trying to decide if it would be astonishingly nerdy to whip it out, or whether not whipping it out to save face would mean a lost opportunity.

Or maybe he was debating whether I was going to make him break it. I wouldn't put it past him to hold a grudge about that.

Finally he dug into his beat-up canvas backpack and pulled out the device. He kept it low, almost beneath the table, as he switched it on. He looked at me.

I inclined my head in both directions. "Pick one," I said.

He chose his right, my left, first. Asia.

"He's kinda cute, in a geeky, unkempt way," Asia said, preening. I was startled that she knew the word "unkempt," much less that she could use it correctly in a sentence.

"Hush," I said.

Rudy jerked back.

"Not you," I said. "Sorry. Go on."

Jesus, what was Asia seeing in Rudy? I mean, he was okay, but she was usually rambling about Evan or Lamar Tinibu. Was she that desperate for attention?

Rudy frowned at the readings, then moved the EMF detector in the other direction. Apparently satisfied with the readings, he shut the thing off and stowed it away.

"The readings are inconsistent, which means an unexplained flux in an electromagnetic field," he said. "But that could mean anything. A bundle of wires running under the floor, for example...."

"Oh, come on," I said. "Of course there could be wires, but do you really think I crawled beneath a Baja Fresh and made sure this exact table was free so I could give you questionable readings? For crying out loud. This is Maggie, and this is Asia."

His head whipped to the left. "Asia *McBride*?"

"The one and only. She's pleased to meet you, by the way."

"Why is she here?" His voice dropped to a whisper.

"Why are you whispering?" I whispered back.

"I don't know," he said in a normal tone. "Why not?"

I knew I'd been snarky, and I already felt bad about it. "I was at the party where Asia died, and since I could see her spirit form, she came with me back to the Ballington. Like I said, you were right—there *are* ghosts there. Several. I'll introduce you to all of them. They help me with my tours, but that's it; I don't use any Hollywood effects."

He had been leaning forward; now he sat back in his chair. "I was right," he repeated.

"You were totally right," I agreed. "Go you."

I let him savor that warm fuzzy while I went through my lime-jalapeño-bite routine with my burrito.

"Your grandfather, Aaron, was part of my tour, too," I added after I'd devoured the bite of heaven. "He really loved the cemetery, you know?" I said. "That's why he stayed around. He took a lot of pride in keeping the grounds tidy. He had his own special rake, wouldn't let anybody else use it. He *hated* it when anyone didn't show the proper respect. 'Take off your farshiltn hat,' he would say. 'Show some respect.'"

As I talked, I was reminded how much I missed Aaron. Aaron, of all ghosts, whom I barely knew. But it's like someone you care about dying, I suppose—you regret not taking the time to know them better.

I was going to find—and kick the ever-living daylights out of—Big Bad Exorcist, not just for Marla, but for Aaron, too. I owed him that.

"That's cool that you knew him," he said. "He was a great guy. I miss him."

"Me, too," I said honestly.

He drank some of his soda.

"So," he said finally. "You said you can see ghosts. How?"

I gave him the basic explanation. He seemed...deflated. Which for him, was saying a lot.

"You don't need equipment," he said. A statement, not a question, but I nodded anyway. "You just...*see* them." He sighed. "That rocks. I wish I would've been able to talk to my grandfather the way you did."

Oh, guilt. "I understand," I said. I did. I wished my grandmother had stuck around a while longer.

A Baja Fresh employee, a young Hispanic girl with gorgeous shiny brown hair, wandered by, desultorily pushing a mop across the floor. I gave her a brilliant smile, because I learned a long time ago that being obvious was entirely less obvious than trying to look like you didn't want to be noticed. Her face lit up as she smiled back.

Rudy pushed the cardboard plate containing the remains of his quesadilla away. "Now," he said, "what exactly do you need help with?"

TWENTY

I DIDN'T KNOW when Tabitha would contact me—I assumed she'd keep her word, but not how long it would take her to get information, and I wanted to talk to Sam again. I needed to know why Otter thought it was so important I bring her in to this.

I mixed myself a shaker of Cosmos and poured one over ice into a martini glass. The stunning ruby liquid glimmered in the slanting sunbeams of early evening. No doubt this is why the parlor was put on this side of the hotel—to enhance the pre-dinner cocktail hour.

For Sam I fixed a whisky, neat. He said he didn't care about the brand, but I'd noticed he appreciated the good stuff, so I kept it on hand for him. Hey, it's hard for a ghost to get visceral pleasures. After the other night, I was swearing off whisky for a while.

Sam, in the leather wing chair, accepted the whiskey dubiously, thanking me because he was that type of person even as he worried about my ulterior motive. I'd already given him the dreaded "we need to talk" speech; he wasn't entirely unaware of what was coming.

I sat on the love seat across from him.

"I know you don't want to talk about this," I said. "And believe me, I wouldn't be asking you if I didn't think it was vitally important. I need to know about Tabitha, Sam. I need to know what happened to her. Start anywhere."

Sam swirled the whiskey in his glass. I waited. When he'd apparently decided, he took a long, decisive swallow.

"Her career had started to slow down," Sam said. "Nobody was admitting that yet, least of all Tabby, but somehow she still knew. First it was less-than-stellar reviews of her latest film, then the films themselves came fewer and farther between. She'd always been a workaholic, and the studio had banked on that."

"A workaholic party girl?" I asked. Wow. When did she find the time?

"She was amazing," Sam said. "She sometimes slept only a few hours a night. When she latched on to something, she just didn't let go, whether it was a movie shoot or planning an elaborate party. She worked closely with her clothing designers to create the perfect gowns for her. That sort of thing."

"So what happened?"

"Things started to slow down before she was ready for them to. Suddenly she had more time on her hands. She kept throwing the parties, going to parties, but then the invitations weren't as frequent. It happened gradually; she didn't quite see it coming. She'd think the lack of an invitation was an oversight, that something had gotten lost in the mail."

I sipped my tart-sweet Cosmo. "How were you involved, Sam? Don't tell me you weren't. When I mentioned the Ballington..."

"I investigated her death, like I told you," he said. "I was never convinced that there wasn't some sort of foul play, something else going on."

"There's more to it than that," I said. "You're holding out on me. She knew you were here at the Ballington, and it freaked her out. Sounds to me like you two knew each other before she died. Plus, you call her Tabby—sounds pretty intimate to me."

Sam stared at me for a long time. He didn't move except for an occasional twitch in his jaw and the way his eyes scanned my face. With his craggy, angular face and surprisingly intense blue eyes, he'd been a handsome man—he was still killer, even if he was almost as old as my dad. (Well, Sam was that age when he died; now he was technically over a hundred.)

When Sam looked away for a second, it was all I could do not to crow "I made you blink!" and do a booty dance of success.

He gave a short laugh. "You think you can out-wait the seasoned PI, eh?"

I gave a tiny shrug and smiled modestly. "I watch a lot of old movies," I said. "Plus I read somewhere that if you want somebody to talk, you've gotta shut up, because eventually they'll feel like they have to fill the silence."

He laughed again. "You've got a second career waiting for you if you want it, Nikki. You could carry on my legacy."

I wasn't sure what my first career was—mediocre actress? Movie mogul's daughter? Will-party-for-pay girl?—but that didn't matter. "Stop trying to flatter me, Sam," I said. "I'm not trying to upset you, but Otter thinks Tabitha is the key to this thing, and if I don't understand what's freaking her out about you or the hotel—and I think it's you—then I might never get the chance to find out what she knows."

"I don't understand how Tabby can be the key," Sam said.

"Neither do I," I said. "But the more I know, the better chance I have of figuring it out."

Sam nodded, his face grave. "Back then, the studio owned you. They decided what pictures you'd be in, even create them for you to star in. That didn't mean you had any input, though. You were just their employee, their property. Did you know Olivia de Havilland had to sue her studio? She asked for roles that weren't as the ingénue, they wouldn't give 'em to her, so she took some time off, and then they expected her to work double-time to catch up."

I wanted to give him the time he needed, but I was getting frustrated. I held up my half-finished Cosmo to cut him off. "Thank you for the history lesson, but you're stalling."

"Is it that obvious?" His tone was rueful.

"Yes. Let me get you another drink."

I poured another whisky for him. Sam knocked back another hefty swallow, apparently fortifying himself. Apparently when ghosts interact with the real world—drinking, banging into something, whatever—they feel the effects as they did when they were alive—getting drunk, raising a bruise, whatever.

They just couldn't stay corporeal for very long; at least, the more they interacted, the more difficult it became. Sam chose to put the glass down between sips. Sitting in a chair was just a formality.

"The studio owned Tabby," Sam said, "and they hired me. My first introduction into the world of Tabitha St. Claire happened because I'd been hired to investigate her."

Whoa. I'd assumed their relationship was personal. "Investigate her for what?"

Sam swirled the remaining whisky in his glass, contemplating the amber alcohol. "If you were the studio's property, your life belonged to them. Oh, it wasn't like it is now, with scandals being posted to the Internet five seconds after they break, with paparazzi stalking a star's every move. Liz Taylor didn't start working through her husbands until the fifties; most stars kept a low profile before that."

I resisted the urge to make a "go on" motion. Scandal?

"They'd noticed that Tabitha took a few days off between movies—up to a couple of weeks, even—and that sometimes she seemed distracted. Or she wouldn't answer her phone during that time. Someone would say she wasn't at home, or indisposed. They wanted me to find out if anything was going on."

"Was there?" I had to know. Not just because I was dying of curiosity for some juicy gossip, but because I needed to know.

He heaved a sigh. "Not that would affect anybody but Tabitha, really. After her fourth film, she'd taken a bit of a break—gone to Europe, the story was, to enjoy her success and taken a vacation. Back then, it wasn't a big deal to take a few months to travel around the world.

"Problem was, she wasn't traveling around the world. She'd gone home to Bakersfield."

"Ah," I said. "She was pregnant."

Sam blinked in surprise. "How did you know?"

"It's not quite a cliché, but really—a woman takes five or so months off? Extended European cruise, working on her memoirs? Nah, she's hiding out so she doesn't show."

"I suppose, looking back now, it's obvious," Sam said. "But things were...more innocent then. It wasn't, as you call it, a cliché."

What must it have been like, I wondered, to laugh and

drink and dance at glittering Hollywood parties while your heart was back home in some small town with a baby you couldn't get to know too well?

At least nowadays it was the chic thing to pop out a few kids, whether you were uber-mama Angelina or still in your teens like the Real Teen Housewives. Pregnancy a scandal? Not so much.

But not only had Tabitha not been able to be with her child, she'd had to hide the truth from all her friends. Protect a secret, unable to share.

Like I didn't know anything about *that*. For me, seeing ghosts was the new secret baby. I doubted *that* would become a cliché decades from now.

"So what happened after you gave your report to the studio?" I asked. "I didn't see anything in Tabitha's bio about a scandal."

"I didn't tell them," Sam said.

I nearly dropped my drink. I didn't have to say anything; he could tell from my reaction what I was thinking.

"I violated my professional code of ethics and lied to an employer," he said. His voice was steady. He'd been living with this for a long time. Well, not *living* with it, exactly, but you know what I mean. "Tabby hadn't done anything wrong. She wasn't in violation of her studio contract. She wasn't taking extra time off, and when she was on set, she gave her work her full focus. The only time she didn't was when her son was ill and she was worried."

"Did she know that you knew?"

He nodded. "I told her, in case the studio didn't believe my report and decided to hire someone else."

"That must've been tough," I said.

"She felt as if she couldn't go home," Sam said. "And that's when it did start affecting her, but only a little."

"So she was mad at you for fucking things up?" I asked.

"No," Sam said. "She was actually grateful that she had someone she could be honest with. We...we became friends."

I would've bet the Ballington that there was more to that statement, but I wasn't sure if it was relevant right now. "Clearly something happened to change that."

"Someone else *did* find out," Sam said. "I don't know who. But Tabby believed it was me. She blamed me for letting the secret out. It wasn't made public, but rumors started."

"And that's why she stopped being invited to parties," I said. The light dawns.

"She didn't know that at first," Sam said. "People just started distancing themselves from her, and her popularity at the box office dropped, and..." He had picked up his drink, and now faded a little, but caught himself before he dropped his drink for real. He took a hefty swallow of whisky and set the empty glass down.

"She was livid," he went on. "She couldn't believe that it wasn't me who did it. She was sure anyone else would've told the studio, would've waved proof at the media. I had no reason to do it, but she just didn't see that."

"That sucks," I said.

"I tried to find out who'd leaked the secret, but I never did," Sam said. "I think it was one of her so-called friends. But without proof, she'd never have believed me about that, either. The whole thing may have had something to do with her death; I just can't prove that, either."

Hell of a way to spend eternity, worrying at an unsolved mystery that had taken away someone you cared about. I'd thought Sam hung around because he was comfortable at the Ballington, but maybe I had been seeing only part of the picture.

"What happened to her son?" I wondered aloud.

"When the rumors started, I sent Tabitha's sister an anonymous donation," Sam said. "Everything the studio had paid me. If it hadn't been for me, maybe nobody would have found out. I don't know if someone followed me or retraced my steps. After Tabby died, I sent more money, but it was returned. They'd moved and hadn't left a forwarding address."

"They were probably benefactors of her estate, weren't they?" I asked.

"No doubt," he said. "But I still felt I should do something."

If I could've hugged Sam, I would've. Instead, I just said, "You know what? After all this is over, let's find out what happened to him. You, me, and the magical power of the Internet."

He smiled then, for the first time since we'd started talking. For the first time, maybe, since I'd brought the notion of Tabitha St. Claire back into his life. "I'd like that," he said. "And if Tabby has to come here, I'll stay out of the way, okay? You tell her that—she doesn't have to worry about seeing my face."

"That's won't be necessary," said a new voice. A sexy, husky one.

Tabitha St. Claire had come to the Ballington.

Sam's form shimmered as if he were trying to decide whether to stay or go. He was normally so strong, so grounded, that it hurt to see him this way.

I'd never been in love, not really. Not like the two of them obviously had been. So I'd never experienced the heartache they were going through. I just hoped somebody looked at me someday the way they were looking at each other.

"Don't leave," Tabitha said to him. "I heard what you said. We have so much to talk about. But first"—and she turned to me—"you and I must talk."

I nodded. I got up and refreshed Sam's drink, thinking he might need it. He nodded his thanks, but although his fingers tightened around the glass, he didn't pick it up.

Tabitha settled gracefully into another armchair. I offered her a drink, but she declined. Meanwhile, the other hotel ghosts arrived: Curtis, with his ever-present headphones around his neck; Asia, looking half miffed and half interested; and finally Janie, strolling through the door as was her preference to filtering. Maggie, of course, had been with me all along.

I realized I was waiting for Marla, and sucked in a shaky breath, blinking back tears.

I introduced Tabitha to the people she hadn't met, and thanked her again for coming. "I'm guessing from your expression that it's not good news," I said.

Somberly, she shook her head. Then, at least she started with the good news.

Marilyn was still fine, thank goodness. The drag queen who had run The Glitter Room with his still-living drag queen sibling was fine too. I sighed with relief; I was fond of her.

But along with Aaron, Thomas and Bertha, and Marla, there was LuAnn over at the Shell station on Fairfax, that surfer I'd never gotten the name of, and the usher at the Staples Center who loved music so much, he never, ever wanted to leave.

A wave of icy surf washed over me. The ghosts all had at least one thing in common.

They all knew me.

So that meant it was highly likely that whoever was doing this also knew me. Maybe knew about the ghosts because of me.

Who would that be? I hadn't told many people. Rudy, who didn't seem to have a motive, but I could be wrong about that. Ned, who didn't believe me to the extent that he'd essentially stopped talking to me. Bridget, maybe, but only if Solange had told her about everyone. Belinda Kelly and Line Braxton, who'd benefitted when I'd helped the ghost of 70s rocker Ricky Linn track down a rare, unpublished song. Neither of them had any motive I could fathom.

Those were the living people. I supposed there was also a chance another ghost was doing it, and maybe targeting me? But why?

Tabitha had helped, but the information wasn't enough. It was just a new piece in the puzzle.

The most important thing was, I had to keep my friends safe.

TWENTY-ONE

RUDY SHOWED up with stacks of cases and duffel bags, all mismatched but bearing the Ominous Spiritus logo. He looked like he was going on a six-month European tour or something. I took pity on him and helped him haul all the shit in. Thankfully I'd had him park in the alley; I could only imagine what people would think if they saw the equipment.

They'd probably think I'd really gone over the edge.

Asia, on the other hand, acted like she wouldn't mind if he were her new secret lover. She didn't help with the trunks and cases and gear, of course. She just followed him in and out like a love-struck puppy, maintaining a running commentary that he couldn't hear.

Of course, he couldn't see her, either, but that didn't stop her flipping her hair and pouting in what she no doubt thought was a provocative manner. I rolled my eyes so far back I almost lost them in the back of my head, but she didn't notice.

Rudy set up a couple of laptops and big monitors in the butler's pantry, a room off the kitchen normally used for storing dishes and prepping food. Because I didn't have an entire hotel to feed, the built-in wooden glass-fronted cabinets were empty, and the massive wooden prep table, scratched and scored from decades of chopping, had nothing on it but a power drill that I'd been looking for.

It made the room look like a beginner serial killer's hideout. I put the drill in a drawer, which meant I'd never find it again.

We could run extension cords through to the kitchen, where there were enough outlets—the kitchen was the first place I'd had properly wired.

"So what did you find out about exorcism?" I asked, impatient, as he fiddled with cords and connections.

He reached out with one hand and tapped at one of the computers. Files flashed up on the screen.

"Exorcism is done on living people," he said. "It's used to drive out an evil spirit or demon, sometimes considered to be the devil himself. In other words, the person is possessed and the possessing entity needs to be removed."

"What about exorcism on a building?" I asked. "Like poltergeists?"

"That's a common misconception," he said. He didn't have to look at his research to pontificate about this aspect of things. He almost sounded authoritative, and I wasn't the only one who noticed. Asia sighed heavily and propped her chin in her hand and, I swear to God, batted her eyelashes.

"Poltergeists aren't actual spirits or ghosts," he went on. "The energy is the manifestation of the transition from adolescence through puberty, generally restricted to girls. The physical and hormonal changes channel into uncontrolled psychic energy. For example—"

"Okay, okay," I said. "Poltergeists have nothing to do with this, I get it."

"The other kinds of ghosts include spirits who don't know they're dead and keep doing the same repetitive motion, like walking down the same hallway, spirits who have unfinished business, possessing spirits..."

"That doesn't fit anyone who's been taken," I said, frustrated. "They weren't repetitive, they didn't have unfinished business, they weren't harming anyone, weren't giving off any negative energy or influence. Your grandfather wasn't *haunting* the cemetery. He was *keeping it tidy*."

Rudy pushed his glasses up his nose. "I know," he said. "Something different is going on here."

I resisted the urge to scream and wrap my hands around his throat and shake him until his head flopped back and forth like a Muppet's. "No shit, Sherlock," I said between gritted teeth. "Have you found any information that might actually pertain to our problem?"

"Well," he said. "Well." He blinked rapidly. I think I'd scared him. Heh. Good. "One thing we know is that even if the ghosts didn't all live here, they were all connected to you. They were part of your tour. Could anyone who's gone on your tour been responsible?"

That would have been a nightmare to figure out. Thankfully, I had an answer. "Not everyone who's been taken was on the tour," I said. "And I never talked about anyone who wasn't on the tour."

"Okay," Rudy said. "Next question: Does Hollywood Forever have security cameras?"

I mentally smacked myself so hard, my mental head wobbled. "I hadn't even thought of that! Let me ping them and see." I had a good relationship with them, because I'd had to negotiate to bring tours through and my tour groups didn't harm anything—I made sure of that.

"In the meantime, I'd like to examine the area where the ghost—your friend Marla—was taken."

I led the way to the solarium, texting as I walked. Janie hadn't done any work here since Marla's exorcism (or whatever you want to call it), and the plants were looking droopy and sad and brown. I totally didn't blame Janie for not wanting to be in here, though. I barely wanted to walk through the doors.

Screw it. I could always buy new plants someday.

I blinked against the bright sunlight streaming through the glass roof panels, a beam illuminating the center of the bench like a spotlight on a prima ballerina. The place looked so bright and inviting. That felt wrong, somehow.

Rudy had lugged in a variety of detectors and sensors and other machines, including a brand new EMF reader.

"Are there any ghosts in here?" he asked.

I couldn't help but snicker, because all of them had trailed after us. Janie and Sam stood in the doorway, but Asia was so close to him I was surprised he wasn't getting frostbite on his left elbow.

And then there was Curtis, who'd responded to the question by moonwalking back and forth in front of Rudy. He'd had decades to perfect his moves, and he was quite proud of them.

"Um, yes," I said.

Behind his glasses, his eyes widened with excitement. He held the EMF up in front of him, chest height and an arm's length away.

Curtis leaned in as if it were a microphone. "Because I'm bad, I'm bad, ow!"

The numbers in the readout screen blurred as they shot up.

"Oh my God," Rudy whispered. "It's right *there*."

"That's Curtis," I said.

"What's he doing?"

"A reasonable impression of Michael Jackson's falsetto," I said. "But I promised you ghost access *after* you'd helped me out. So, chop chop."

Rudy sighed. "I'm just trying to verify that my equipment is working."

He set up some hidden digital cameras around the perimeter, pointing at the bench and also at the door. They'd continue to record and we could review the video any time we wanted, he said.

Then he set up other equipment, muttering to himself, trailing wires. Asia followed him around, asking questions until she remembered he couldn't hear her. Then she just leaned close to watch.

"Back off and let him work," I said. "If you're too close, you'll screw up the results."

She stuck her lower lip out in a pout, but retreated with the rest of us. Rudy, brow furrowed, opened his mouth to ask, but apparently thought the better of it and went back to work.

He crouched down and examined the bench, running the EMF above it in slow, regular sweeps. Went around behind it, did the same. Then he walked in ever-widening circles, EMF-ing the brick floor and the air and, as he got close to them, potted ferns.

Ooh, those evil ferns. I bit my lip and asked for patience. Right now, please.

He knelt down again, head cocked. He touched his fingers to the ground, sniffed them, then touched them to his tongue. Ew, WTF?

"Has anyone else been in here since the exorcism?" he asked, standing.

"My friend Solange," I said. "She a psychic—very powerful. She examined the area as well, and is going to consult with her spirit guide."

"What did she do, exactly, when she examined the area?"

I tried to remember. I'd been pretty upset and, if memory served, had had a few shots of something nice and strong. "She raised a circle, did some sort of ritual."

"Salt?" He held up his fingers. I could see white granules on the tips.

"And a sage smudge, some kind of holy water, and..." There'd been something else. "A bell."

"Did she say why she raised a circle?"

"I didn't know I should've asked." He was getting on my nerves again. "I assume she was protecting the area because she'd be vulnerable when she was trying to figure out what had been there."

"Well, maybe..." He didn't look convinced. "I don't know a lot about Wicca, so I can't be sure until I do a little more research. But it looks to me like what she did was a cleansing ritual."

I frowned. "Well, doesn't that make sense? I mean, if there was negative stuff—energy or whatever—she'd want to clear it out."

"I suppose," he said. "The problem is, she cleaned away most of the traces of what actually happened. I don't think there's much left for me to find."

"Well, crap," I said.

"You said she raised a circle," he said. "Is that all she drew with the salt and stuff?"

I squinted, thinking. "I don't remember anything else."

"Did you or anyone else come in here and, I dunno,

sweep the floor or walk around this area a lot, that sort of thing."

"I was in here last night... No, I wasn't." That had been a dream. I glanced over at my ghosts. They all shook their heads. "Nobody," I said. "Not since Solange was here—the same night you were."

"Huh. Do you have a ladder?" he asked, which I so did not expect. I figured it was best not to ask why.

"I've got a step stool in the kitchen," I said. "I'll be right back."

He set the thing up right in front of the bench, climbed up, took a picture of the floor. Stepped down, turned the steps forty-five degrees, did it again. He repeated the process until he'd covered a whole circle.

What the hell was he doing?

I found out a few minutes later when he hopped down and charged for the dining room. Asia and I were hot on his heels (for entirely different reasons, and if she made one comment about his ass, I was going to figure out a way to trip her, I swear); the others trailed behind.

He dumped the photos into one of the laptops and fiddled with them in some programs. Then he turned the laptop towards me and showed me how he'd arranged them.

Despite having been swept away by Solange, some salt had stuck in the grooves and pits of the tile flooring. The original painted ceramic tiles were gorgeous, still, even after decades of abuse and neglect. The salt in the cracks and chipped-out areas wasn't really visible when you were standing there, but from above, you could see where the white spots were.

Put together, you could see that the salt had once been poured to form a pattern. Not just a circle. No, there were lines and swirls and squiggles. Enough had been swept away that I couldn't entirely tell what exactly the design had been.

"I'll be damned," I said. "What is it?"

"I don't know yet," Rudy said. "I wanted to get it all photographed and arranged so I could compare it to different symbols and see if I can ID it. I don't think it's Wiccan. Maybe alchemical." He looked at me over the top of his glasses. "You told me she'd just raised a circle."

"I never saw her do all that," I protested. "All I saw was the circle."

"Are you sure?"

"She was only here the once, and that's all I saw her do. Maybe that symbol was already there." I had a major *duh* moment. "Maybe it was done by the person who exorcised Marla!"

"That's a distinct possibility," he said, nodding. "There's no easy way to tell if the salt used in the circle is the same as the stuff in the symbol."

"What, you don't have a CSI kit in all that stuff?" Ooh, *CSI: Paranormal*. That would be a neat show. I'd have to tell my dad. Wait, wait, *CSI: Salem*! Totally there.

"Not really," he said. "Haven't needed it. But if you didn't see Solange create the symbol, then she didn't do it, right? Nobody else had been in the room since she cleansed it."

"Not unless somebody broke in. It must have happened before—Rudy, you're a genius! That's a direct clue to who did it! That's—"

I stopped. I didn't want to say it was more than Solange had managed to do. It wasn't her fault she was swamped at the store. She had a life; Rudy, as far as I figured, didn't.

"So what else do you know about the symbol?" I asked.

"Only that I was picking EMF readings off of it, so there

was energy attached to it. It's residual, but it's definitely there. Solange's cleansing cleared most of it away."

"She might recognize what the symbol is, what it's used for."

"I'll make you a copy for her," he said.

He stood. "Okay," he said. "I'll be back tomorrow. I've got a lot of data to analyze."

"How long will it take?" I asked as he gathered up some of his stuff.

"A few hours for the basic stuff, but researching that symbol may take some time. I'll look online, but all of my books are at home, so I'll have to pick some of them up."

I saw him out, then went to the kitchen and dug out the second half of my burrito from yesterday, along with the little containers of lime slices and jalapeños. I leaned against the stainless steel island to eat.

For the first time, I felt like we were getting somewhere.

Now I just had to keep everyone intact and on this plane of existence for a little while longer.

TWENTY-TWO

THE NEXT DAY I had another tour in the afternoon. Asia was willing to do a shtick at Hollywood Forever—there was no rake to be found so she settled for blowing cold air on people when they were near Joey Ramone's grave—and Curtis filled in for Marla. During tea at the Ballington, someone noticed the equipment in the solarium and I truthfully told them it was ghost-hunting gear from a local unit doing research. It kind of added to the atmosphere, I realized. Maybe I'd pick up some fake stuff later.

After I dropped them back off, I picked up pizzas (chicken, artichoke, and garlic for me, good ol' pepperoni for Solange), and she and I curled up in the small living room space of my suite on the third floor to watch the AAMies. (That red monstrosity of Shay Constanza's? What *had* her stylist been thinking? She looked like a helium balloon in high heels.)

The ghosts stayed away. They weren't fond of Solange, especially Janie. I had made them promised to report in at regular intervals, though, because I was nervous for them.

Before she left, Solange made me promise to drink the

tisane. Despite everything, I'd been sleeping fine. (It's too bad they don't have jobs for professional sleepers, because I could rake it in.) I told her as much, but she reminded me that it was also designed to help me dream.

That got me thinking. Rudy was on the case, Solange was doing her thing, Tabitha had brought information... what was I doing? Not a whole lot, it felt like. So I promised to take it that very night, and after we finished watching the show and I walked her out to her car—she was headed to Star Dust to do inventory, poor thing—I went straight to the kitchen and put on the kettle.

I checked my email while waiting for the water to boil.

Tour stuff, spam...something from Hollywood Forever.

The file I'd requested, it said, was attached.

As much as I wanted to watch the security camera recording right there on my phone, I knew the small screen would make identifying anyone close to impossible. My best bet would be Rudy's massive monitor—if I knew how to work his setup, which I most certainly did not.

"Hello?" His voice sounded bleary when he answered my call.

I told him I had the recording. To his credit, he said, "I'm guessing you want me to come over right now."

"Got it in one. Thanks," I added before I disconnected and dealt with the screaming kettle.

I PACED UNTIL RUDY ARRIVED, sipping my hot, minty tasting drink.

Rudy brought up the picture on the enormous monitor he'd set up.

"Do you know what time it happened?" he asked.

"Not a clue," I said. "I can tell you when the last time I saw Aaron was, and then when I found out he was gone. I'd guess that it happened sometime after hours, if the person who did this had to perform some sort of ceremony or ritual."

The screen was split into four views: the front gate viewed from the tiny guard shack, the side service entrance gate, the small mausoleum in the pond viewed from the big mausoleum, and the big mausoleum, from a tree, maybe?

Bingo! The shot from the big mausoleum towards the pond illuminated the grassy area between the Warren Wilson's slab and the small Cutts mausoleum where we'd always hook up with Aaron on the tour.

My elation depleted the longer nothing happened; even though we were going at triple speed, I swear we watched grass grow. It was hardly fascinating. A duck waddling over the lawn should *not* have been such a cause for celebration.

The area I was so familiar with looked eerie and disconcerting in grainy black-and-white. The fountains in the lake were off; the place looked...dead. Sorry, but it did.

"By the way," Rudy said, "I did some digging on that Tabitha St. Claire you told me about." I'd been texting him to fill in details and keep him updated.

"And?"

"I found an old book that suggested she'd told her best friend, who ratted her out in exchange for money. Maybe the studio bribed her after Sam walked off the case."

I started to say, "That makes sense," but Rudy interrupted me.

"What's that?" He leaned forwards to peer at the screen. "Is that an entity?"

"I think it's a flashlight."

The person wore loose clothes and a hoodie pulled up,

obscuring not only their figure but their face as well. All we could tell was that they was reasonably tall and not excessively bulky.

As we watched the grainy black-and-white camera recording, the person poured a big ol' circle of salt, then began adding scribings of salt within the circle.

I swear my jaw dropped. Beside me, Rudy murmured, "That's the same symbol we found in the atrium. That proves it's the same person."

All of a sudden I didn't want to watch. My stomach roiled in protest of all the junk food and the stress, making me deeply regret that last slice of pizza. I sipped my tea. I wanted to run and bury my face in Grandma Rosa's lap like I did when I was a kid and a scary movie was on.

Sucks being a grown-up.

I hadn't fully seen what had happened to Marla. I'd gotten impressions, brief snapshots, from Sam somehow while it was going on. It didn't surprise me that ghosts might have some sort of telepathic communication, or that I could tune into that fuzzy channel when they projected it at me.

Suffice to say the bits I'd seen of Marla had been painful enough. She'd clutched the cushion, begged for help, terrified.

I doubted Aaron had wanted to go any more than Marla had. And now I was going to have to watch it from start to finish.

The video had been running while we talked, and now the figure had completed the intricate symbol. He set out four fat candles and lit them, then walked counterclockwise around the outside of the circle with what looked to be a sage smudge.

"Widdershins," Rudy said.

"What?" I asked.

"Counterclockwise is also called widdershins. In Wicca and some other traditions, it's used for grounding energy."

That seemed...backwards. "Not raising it?"

"The idea is that clockwise, or deosil, raises the energy and widdershins grounds it again," said my little font of arcane information. He and Solange would have a blast with each other. "But that's for white magick. If this is some sort of black magick, maybe it's done the opposite way."

"Like how Satanists use the upside-down pentagram?"

"Like that, yeah," Rudy agreed. "And the candles look like they're some dark color, maybe black."

I swallowed against the heartburn and nerves. The figure, facing away from the camera and thus still unidentifiable to us, raised both arms in the air, hands open and then fisted, then brought them down in a sharp, commanding gesture. There was a flash, not exactly of light, but of something suddenly appearing...

...and then the person performing the ritual fuzzed out, as if someone had smeared Vaseline over the camera lens. Only it was just over the person, not the whole scene. Like on *Star Trek* when someone started to beam up, when the sparkles of light were still in human form, before they faded away.

"What the—" Rudy hit pause, backed up the recording, played it again.

As the same thing happened, I said, "I'll bet you anything that's what it looks like when Donny tries to take a picture of me when the ghosts are around me. I'll bet it's not the recording."

"Who's Donny?" Rudy asked.

"My personal paparazzo. Long story," I said. I looked at the screen. "So Aaron must be there," I said sadly. "Can you back up again? I want to see it frame-by-frame."

"Sure." Rudy set the scene to where the figure brought his hands down, and brought it forwards slowly.

"There," I said, and he paused it again. "Go back, like, one or two frames." I pointed at the beginnings of an indistinct form, a ghost who wasn't quite all there yet. By the next frame he'd be obscured, a victim of his own ability to mess up visual recording equipment. "That's Aaron."

"What is?" Donny asked.

"That right there." I stabbed my finger at the screen, circled the see-through, misty human-shaped form.

Rudy swallowed. "That's my grandfather?"

"I assume it's him," I said. "I can't tell for sure, but who else would it be? Are you sure you want to watch this?"

He blew out a breath of air. "I've already said goodbye to him," he said finally. "And I only found out he was a ghost a few days ago—a ghost I probably couldn't have communicated with. So I'm okay. Thanks for asking."

We continued to view at normal speed—not that there was much to see. The blurred figure didn't move much, so for two minutes and eighteen seconds we watched a stationary blob in a still setting.

Still, I hugged my arms around myself. I knew what was happening, even if I couldn't see it. Aaron might not have reacted exactly as Marla had, but he'd probably have felt fear and anger and helplessness as he flickered in and out, unable to fight what was being done to him. Ripping him away from his connection to the earth. Had he fought, pled, cried out for help that couldn't come?

"I wish we had audio," Rudy said. "I'd give anything to hear the details of the ritual. That would help determine what belief system or magickal practice it's from."

He sounded genuinely curious, and that surprised me. I thought he'd be more emotional about the whole thing. But,

I realized, Rudy was a scholar—even if this was about his grandfather, he would be dispassionate when it came to the scientific research aspect of the situation.

Well, insofar as paranormal research is "scientific." YMMV.

The figure moved his arms, and *I* saw a flash of that *something* again, which I assumed Rudy couldn't see, and then the fuzziness was gone and the person was alone and as clear as the grainy security footage could make them.

They still managed to keep their face obscured by the hood as they scuffed out the symbols in the grass and snuffed out the candles. When they picked up the bag to store the candles and empty salt bag, I found myself leaning forwards, squinting at the screen.

Something looked really familiar, but I couldn't put my finger on it. It niggled in the back of my brain.

"Can you zoom in on the bag?"

The scene magnified and re-resolved. The graininess was worse, but not so bad that I couldn't make out what I needed.

I hadn't recognized the logo in black and white, because I was used to seeing it in purple and gold.

Star Dust.

"Sonovabitch," I said.

The recording moved forwards. Rudy zoomed back out. We still couldn't see the person's face, but as they picked up their things and walked briskly off-screen, I saw all the hints I hadn't clued in to before.

Clearly Rudy did, too, because he said, "Is that a woman?"

"It is." It was hard to talk; I realized I was clenching my teeth.

I sat back, every muscle in my body taut with rage.

Rudy let the video run on. His voice seemed to come from far away. "Nikki, do you recognize her?"

The hair and that confident stride, combined with the Star Dust bag. Damn straight I recognized her.

Bridget.

I should've known.

TWENTY-THREE

I WOKE up sprawled on my back on my bed, fully clothed, groggy and disoriented, my mouth tasting like something awful. Kimchi, maybe. That's never a good sign.

I patted my hand on my night table until I found my iPhone. It was 3:42 a.m. A time when people would be staggering home from clubbing, photographers snapping them as they poured themselves into cars, makeup smeared and clothes rumpled.

Why was I awake?

Why hadn't I changed into pajamas like a normal person?

I sat up, and discovered I had one Van on. That brought back a memory, slowly, as if my brain was pushing it through that slime they dump on you at that kids' awards show. I'd been...going somewhere.

To confront Bridget.

I'd come upstairs to put on my shoes and call Solange. Had I called Solange? I looked at my phone. Didn't look like it. I clearly hadn't managed to get both of my shoes on, much less leave the hotel.

The tisane. Bridget *had* tampered with it. She'd *poisoned* me.

Somewhere beneath the grogginess, I felt really, really angry.

I flicked on the beaded lamp beside my bed, but nothing happened. Electricity must be out—not an unusual occurrence in this old place, although I'd spent a fortune having electricians crawl around trying to find the problems

I called Solange's cell, but she didn't answer. Then I remembered she was doing inventory all night. I found Star Dust in my contacts, tapped the number to call. When a voice said, "Hello?" I said, "Solange, it's me. Bridget is the one exorcising the ghosts."

It took me three times to get my tongue to properly enunciate "exorcising." I added, "I think Bridget added something to the tisane, too. I need coffee," and I hung up.

Funny how we still say "hung up" when it's just poking at a screen.

I put on my other shoe and grabbed the flashlight I always keep by the bed.

As I headed down the hall to the stairs by the beam of my flashlight, a thought pushed its way through the heavy layers of grogginess and gripped my throat.

"Maggie? Curtis?" Curtis was usually the night owl. I listened, but heard nothing, not even the soundtrack to *Purple Rain*, which was one of his current favorites. "Anyone?"

I felt overwhelmingly alone. The hotel seemed to expand outside the narrow beam of my flashlight, spreading outwards until I was the only one left in infinite space. Like when you're a kid and you lie on the lawn at night and get bowled over by the stars and the vastness of space.

What? Don't tell me that was only me.

But this was worse than that, because I couldn't run inside my parents' house and find my family and be assured that no, everyone in existence except me had not in fact been swallowed by the universe.

I transferred my phone to my flashlight hand and gripped the dark-stained oak banister as I crept down the wide front stairs. I couldn't even bring myself to call out again. My throat had closed up.

Was this what a panic attack was like? Eden had them, or so she claimed. I always thought she was looking for attention.

Could they all have been exorcised? Was that even possible? It was hard to think straight.

Maybe they were hiding from whatever had woken me up. That made me feel marginally better about them, but a lot more nervous about what might be out there. Er, in here.

My foot skidded on the carpeted edge of a step and only my grip on the bannister kept me from pitching down the staircase. My phone slipped from my fingers and hit the carpeted stair, then I heard it bounce, and then, ages later, another thud. It must have fallen through the railings. Thank goodness I hadn't dropped my flashlight. What was wrong with me? I could barely walk. It was like the time I had hives and took Benadryl and stabbed myself in the face with my fork. Ned had nearly peed himself laughing.

After I got to the lobby and found my phone, I stopped and listened again. A car went by outside. My heart throbbed in my ears.

Maybe I should get a dog. Not some yappy-type thing, but one that would bite an intruder's kneecap. But I didn't even know if I had an intruder. The only person who'd ever broken in was Rudy, and there was no reason for Rudy to break in again, because I'd told him I'd give him access if he helped me.

Oh, and the person who'd exorcised Marla.

Crap.

A lot of maybes, none that were helping me right now, when my world had narrowed to the beam of my flashlight and I didn't know what to do. Yes, I did: I wanted to go back to bed.

Not until I made sure nothing was wrong, though.

That's when I heard something. A low chanting or singing. It was barely there, but it curled up around me like a snake, hugging me in its coils, making me even groggier, if that was possible.

Stubbornly, I still wanted to know where it was coming from.

There was enough ambient light down here that I didn't need the flashlight. Even in my current loopy state, I knew my way around the main floor.

One step in front of the other, I followed the source of the sound, and was somehow not surprised and yet shaking with fear when it led me to the solarium.

One of the wide, frosted glass doors was partway open. I eased inside. The song was definitely louder here.

The person was facing away from me, wearing a dark hoodie with the hood up. Rage surged up inside me through the fog.

"Bridget!"

The person in the solarium turned towards me.

The next thing I knew, the lights were on. Not so much that they came on suddenly—it felt more like they'd always been on and I was just waking up and realizing it.

It was hard to focus my sight. I didn't see anyone in the solarium.

Someone behind me put a hand on my shoulder, and I spun around so fast my feet got tangled up and I nearly fell. I flailed and the flashlight went flying. The person caught me before I went down.

I couldn't process. "Solange? What are you doing here?"

"You called me, *cher*. Don't you remember?"

I struggled for the memory. "Yes, but only a few minutes ago. Right before I came downstairs."

"It was more like three hours ago," she said. "You said you weren't feeling well, that you were scared, and asked me to come over. I just didn't get the message until about forty-five minutes ago, and then I came right over."

"I don't remember," I said. I felt like a little kid, petulant at being woken. "I'm not scared, either. Except I can't find anybody. Where's Maggie? Or Asia? Or...?"

"You tell them not to bother you when you're sleeping, *cher*." Solange's voice was honey-soothing. "Now, why don't we brew you up some of that tisane and get you back to bed?"

"I drank some before I went to bed," I protested. I licked my dry lips. My tongue still tasted icky, which was weird, because the tisane had been minty and comforting.

"Did you?" she asked. "Well, then, maybe you should have a drink. C'mon."

She steered me to the parlor, poured me a couple fingers of whisky.

"Sam usually joins me for a whisky," I mumbled after taking a sip.

"Sam's with Tabitha, remember?"

Was he? I guess did tell Sam they had a lot to talk about. Of course, "We need to talk" was never a good thing, was it?

"I'll have a drink with you," she said, pouring herself some amber liquid. "*Santé*," she said.

"Sure," I said, and took another swallow. Then I put the glass down. My mouth still tasted bad, and the alcohol wasn't helping. "I need some water," I said.

"Well then, let's get you back upstairs to bed, and I'll pour you a glass," she said.

Sleep sounded good. Really good. I could barely keep my eyes open. Maybe I was dreaming? I let her lead me out of the parlor.

As the old elevator rattled its way up, I leaned against the back wall, suddenly too tired to stand. Something flickered out of the corner of my eye, and I glanced left. The bottom half of the elevator walls were papered in rich, gold-flocked brocade, but the top half were mirrored.

I saw my own reflection, my arms hugged across my chest, and then the endless reflections of reflections as they bounced off the mirror across the way. Solange's reflection was farther forwards, because she stood by the controls at the front.

Next to my other me, Janie appeared, her hands out as if she were pressing against something. Her mouth moved, but I couldn't hear her words.

Startled, I looked next to me where she should have been standing. (Ghosts, unlike vampires, do make reflections; in fact, they can sometimes do it better than actually appearing. Which explains a lot about what people report about hauntings, if you think about it.).

She wasn't there.

I pushed away from the wall, swaying unsteadily, as I looked back at the mirror.

She was gone from the mirror, too.

The elevator lurched to a stop and I stumbled.

Solange caught my arm. "Okay, *cher*?"

I didn't bother asking her if she'd seen Janie. Solange

could never see any of them. I didn't understand that. With all her mojo, you'd think she could.

"Solange," I said as we exited the elevator, "why were you in the solarium?"

"Oh, *cher*, you really *are* confused," she said. "When I got here, I found *you* in there."

"What? No." My protest was so weak she didn't even respond. I didn't seem to have any energy, any strength left.

As we stepped out of the elevator, an icy chill numbed my body from the waist down, as if I'd walked through a freezer. As if freezer had walked through me.

"Did you feel that?" I asked.

"Feel what?" Solange asked.

For a brief moment I thought I saw Maggie, which given the height of the chill made sense. Except she wasn't really there.

My last thought was that this wasn't the right hallway.

TWENTY-FOUR

SOMETHING SLID THROUGH MY SHOULDER, so painfully frigid that it felt like my arm would shatter.

I jerked awake. Asia stood over me.

"What the hell?" I said. "Didn't I teach you the no-waking-me rule?"

"You needed to wake up," she said. "Did you take a bunch of drugs again?"

"No, Bridget drugged me," I snapped. Then my brain caught up with my mouth. "Bridget drugged me?"

"Wake up, Nikki!" Asia said, grabbing at my arm again as if trying to yank me up. I batted her away weakly, ineffectually, but I climbed to my feet.

I was not in my bedroom. I was in one of the upper rooms, on a floor I hadn't renovated yet.

Still brain-fogged, I followed Asia to the window and looked out. A three-quarter moon was rising. Only a few stars were visible; the rest were muted by the never-ending lights of LA.

A row of skinny pines bordered the far edge of the hotel's double-sized back yard. Beyond them started a residential area; the first house was low enough that I couldn't see much more than its orange clay barrel tile roof.

Move along, nothing to see here. I looked directly down.

I was over the solarium. I'd never really noticed what a great view of the garden room I had up here. Then again, I didn't come up to this floor on a regular basis. Once it had been determined to be structurally sound, it dropped pretty low on my very loose and mental Things to Clean Up and Generally Repair list. This room, for example, was filled with decades-old detritus: broken bedframes, a washstand with a huge chunk out of its marble top, a pile of water-stained *National Geographics*.

As I looked down, it slowly dawned on me that what I *should* be seeing was the reflection of the city lights on the glass roof.

Instead, what I saw was the solarium lit with flickering points of light. Candle flames, I realized.

But that wasn't what caught my attention—what caught my breath in my throat, made my stomach dropped out as surely as if I was on the roller coaster with Otter. Fuck me, I was awake now.

Glowing lines traced a pattern on the solarium floor. I recognized that pattern. It was the same symbol I'd seen before—only much, much larger, obscured in places by the lush plants and decorative statuary and benches.

It wasn't just the symbol, or the fact that Bridget stood in the middle of it. The horrifying thing was that Janie was in there with her.

I ran to the door. It was locked. I yanked and rattled the doorknob, but just my luck, it was the one thing on this floor that wasn't falling apart.

I also wanted to kill Bridget, so much that it filled me up

and choked me—but I didn't know how. I ran back to the window.

Maggie appeared inside the symbol.

That's when I screamed. So help me God, I screamed louder and better than Jamie Lee Curtis and a sea of tween fans at the latest boy band concert combined.

Down below me, Bridget was waving her hands—she was holding a necklace in one—and creating something glowing of her own in the air in front of her, and then Tabitha was in the circle, too. She and Janie looked like they were trying to protect Maggie.

I couldn't watch anymore. I couldn't be helpless anymore. Whatever drug Bridget had given me had been burned away by anger and fear and their attendant adrenalin. I didn't remember running to the door this time, but I was in front of it again, and this time I had the marble washstand top in my hands.

I'm sorry, dear Ballington.

I slammed the edge of the heavy slab down on the doorknob. The knob broke free of the door, the wood splintering beneath it.

I didn't dare take the elevator. Six flights of stairs down, and halfway there I did spare a moment of thanks to my trainer.

The next flight down, my feet skidded on the carpet and went right out from under me.

I flailed out, caught the banister. Instead of tumbling ass-over-teakettle (as my mother once said when she was drunk) and breaking my freaking neck, I swung around and slammed into the heavy wood. The thick, angled rail hit me from ribcage to hip, driving the air out of me. For a second I felt my feet leave the ground again, and even though it was all going in slow motion—really, not just a movie effect—

and I couldn't quite catch my breath, my stomach lurched and I was sure I was going to pitch over the edge and break my freaking neck that way.

Then my toes touched the ground again, and I collapsed back onto the stairs, gulping for air and light instead of the blackness dimming the edges of my vision.

As soon as I could, I was up again, stumbling down, one step at a time, ignoring the ache in my gut. I wondered if I'd cracked a rib or anything. Frankly, I didn't much care.

I hit the lobby floor and stumbled, my feet forgetting what it's like to run on flat ground. Kinda like when you're a kid and you're running down a hill and you suddenly realize you are totally not in control anymore. I caught myself on the back of a chair, took a deep breath, and careened off towards the back of the hotel.

Bridget was at the door to the solarium.

Wordless rage bubbled out of my throat as I launched myself at her—which, if you think about it, was a pretty gutsy move because she's six-foot-gazillion and could stomp me like Godzilla versus Bambi.

She caught my wrists. "Nikki, stop! I'm not doing this!"

Unfortunately, the race downstairs had exhausted me. Normally it wouldn't have, but normally I don't ingest mystery drugs before I work out.

Y'know, drugs had gotten me into this mess in the first place. Ooh, irony (in the correct sense of the word, not in the Alanis sense of the word).

"The door's locked, Nikki," Bridget went on, breaking through my spinning vision and giving me something to focus on. "I can't get in."

"But you were just in there," I said. "I saw you from upstairs."

Her voice held some gentle emotion I couldn't quite

place. She let go of my arms. "That wasn't me," she said. "I can't be in there and locked out here, too, can I?"

Oh. Um, yeah, that made sense. Plus she wasn't wearing a hoodie, although I supposed she could have stashed it somewhere.

Still... I grabbed the handle of the French doors into the solarium. She was right: Locked. Even though I'd broken the lock when Marla was being taken. Whoever was in there had wedged the doors shut somehow.

This was going to hurt a hell of a lot more than the door upstairs, too. But it was between Maggie (and Janie and Tabitha) and irreplaceable doors, and my friends won out. Duh. I didn't even have to think about the decision.

I gathered myself, took as deep a breath as I could, and slammed my foot into the juncture of the doors in a kick-boxing move that would've done my trainer proud. The doors burst open, slamming against the walls. I heard the glass shatter out of one of them, but I couldn't look. I didn't have time.

The person in the symbol whirled at the intrusion.

For a moment, everything went blank in my brain. Could. Not. Compute. When I came back to myself, I was still suffused with rage, which was a good thing because it helped fill the hollow stabbing pain of betrayal.

She'd been my *friend*.

TWENTY-FIVE

SOLANGE.

As I stood there, gobsmacked, Bridget ran by me and careened to a stop at the edge of the glowing symbol as if she'd smacked into a wall. She staggered back, hand to her forehead. Ouch. A part of me sympathized, even as my brain desperately tried to parse what was going on.

I stepped forwards to where Bridget had hit the invisible barrier. The air glowed faintly, rising up from the salt trail marked on the floor. I knew it was the edge of the symbol. The symbol that had something to do with my friends being exorcised into oblivion.

My friends who were *inside* the symbol with Solange.

I put my hand out. The glow felt solid, and my hand tingled. The type of tingle that I get in the fourth floor ladies' room if I touch the faucet and the light switch at the same time. Not good, in other words. I snatched my hand back, shaking it. No wonder Bridget's head hurt.

Solange spared us a derisive glance before she turned her back on me and continued her chanting. The ghosts, on the other hand, stared at me, eyes full of terror and a desperate plea for help.

Janie screamed. For some reason, I couldn't hear the sound, but it resonated inside me.

"The symbol is what allows her to exorcise the ghosts," Bridget was saying. "I'll try to pull it down."

Bridget obviously wasn't Solange's collaborator, but now I wasn't really sure who, or what, she was. I didn't have time to ask right now, though.

Tears streamed down my face as I watched Curtis grasp at "life" and fail, and fade.

That was it. No more.

The symbol had something to do with raising spirits of the dead, Rudy and Bridget had said. Well, I was all about seeing spirits of the dead, wasn't I? While Bridget was waving her hands around and chanting, not in what I saw as a very effectual manner, I took matters into my own hands. Literally.

Cute sassy little Nikki Ashburne, ex-party girl and failed celebutante, was in quite a violent mood tonight.

I punched at the invisible wall, throwing my entire body weight behind it.

I don't know what I expected—I suppose I was somehow braced to fail and slam into it just like Bridget had. At the very least, that I'd encounter some serious resistance.

Instead, it was like punching through water: it might have slowed me down a little bit, but nothing to write home about. The biggest downside was that the barrier didn't feel like water at all. It felt like an electrical shock. A million and a half bees stung me simultaneously as I fell through, my momentum yanking my whole body along with my fist and arm.

Thankfully the astonishing pain lasted only a second, and my movement was accompanied by a crackling flare of light. Supernova, and then nothing. The glowing symbol circle around us was gone.

My knees smashed against the tiles, but I scrambled to my feet, because there was no way I was going to be on my hands and knees in front of Solange.

I was too late. To my horror, I realized only the two of us were in the middle of the room, what had been the middle of the symbol. The ghosts were gone.

"For fuck's sake, Nikki," Solange said in an accent that didn't contain a trace of Creole, "can't I ever make you just *go away?*"

I regretted not bringing the marble slab with me. It would've had a nice effect on Solange's head.

Speaking of which, in the reflection of the glass wall, I could see Bridget lying by the broken-open French doors. She must've been knocked out by the blast. Dammit. I hoped she was okay.

"I suppose I should thank you," Solange admitted. I stared at her. What the hell? "I needed ghosts to exorcise, and you so kindly provided them. I barely even had to ask." She smiled, and it was ugly, like she was just baring her teeth.

"You...used me?" I knew how stupid I sounded saying it out loud. My voice sounded far away, pathetic. Because I *was* pathetic. The one person I'd trusted more than anyone had completely played me for a fool.

"There are a lot of fakes out there, *cher*," she said. "Lucky for me, I found the real thing."

I wondered if she'd sought me out; if it hadn't been a fortuitous (or so I thought at the time) meeting. But right now, it didn't matter.

Right now, I was getting really pissed.

Keep her talking.

I shook my head. Who said that? The voice was familiar, but too faint to place.

"Are you at least going to tell me why?" I asked. "I'm guessing it's not about just being an ass?"

She snorted. "Don't be more of an idiot than you already are. Of course not. You're not worth just messing with for the fun of it."

Well, that put her in a different category than Eden and Chris, but not necessarily a better one.

"I needed to gather the energy to raise a ghost of my own," Solange said.

"Paul? You did this for love?"

Now she full-out laughed at me, the bitch. The necklace in her hand swayed. I realized it was a medallion bearing the same symbol as on the floor. "You are such a romantic."

She said that like it was a bad thing. Huh.

"He was a good lay," she went on, "and sure, we worked well together. Made a good team. Until he went and died on me before telling me where he'd stashed the money."

"You were going to raise your partner's ghost to make him tell you where some money is?"

"A cool ten mill," she said. "Probably not a lot of money to your rich-family standards, but a fortune to us."

I really, really hated it when people held my father's money over me, as if it was somehow my fault.

"It's not like you can do anything to stop me," she added. "I didn't expect you to wake up, much less get out of the room, but what do you think you can do now?"

Good question. What *could* I do? I wanted to jump her, beat her face into a bloody pulp, but I was pretty sure she could take me right now. I was still weak, and she had height and weight on me. "You're a thief," I said. "You stole that money from somebody, which means someone's looking for you."

"Oh, *right*," she said with a laugh. "You're going to go to the police and say what, exactly? That you see ghosts, and I exorcised them, and now you're angry? You don't have the guts to out yourself."

I opened my mouth to contradict her, but you know what? She was right. Nobody would believe me. It would just earn me another trip to the spa.

"Even if you just said you'd seen me, recognized me, I'll be long gone," Solange said. "And don't worry, I know how to cover my tracks. Besides, with the drugs in your system..."

Craptastic. You bitch. "So, you're just going to walk out of here."

"You going to stop me?"

"No," said another voice. "We are."

The room dropped a good forty degrees between one heartbeat and the next.

Solange apparently couldn't see them, but I could.

The voice had been Sam's, but the first one I saw was Maggie. She was tear-streaked but defiant, as much as a cute blond ringletted little kid could be, and I knew, even with her unable to tell me in so many words, that this had been her doing.

Solange hadn't exorcised her. My heart soared. Instead, Maggie had gone out and gathered the ghosts of Hollywood, a spectral cavalry riding through the ether to my aid.

Sam and Tabitha, although not standing together. Solange hadn't managed to get them, either. Asia, fists on her hips. Marilyn, bless her heart. DiVanita from the Glitter Room. Ghosts I'd met or seen in passing, and ones I'd had no idea were around. A couple of surprising famous faces, but I really didn't have time to do more than think, *Huh, check that out.*

A small but determined lynch mob. A dead mob, though. What could they do?

I had no idea, no concept. In hindsight, I was kind of glad I hadn't known.

I took several quick steps back to get away from them.

Solange had noticed when the temperature had dropped, and she narrowed her eyes at me. "What are you looking at?" she demanded. "You really don't think that tired cliché of—"

It was Tabitha who reached out, wrapped her hand around the leather cord, and yanked the medallion from Solange's hand. *That* got her attention. "What the—"

Without looking away from Solange, Tabitha tossed the medallion aside. I hadn't know her long, but the look in her dark blue eyes—the dead cold fury—sent a shiver through me. The medallion bounced and skittered across the flagstones, coming to rest near me. Without looking away, I knelt and picked it up. I didn't want it, didn't want what it represented, but I felt like I should take it. I couldn't bring anybody back with it, but I couldn't abandon them, either.

Tabitha's actions were an unspoken signal. The mob moved closer to Solange, reaching out, grasping and grabbing for her. Like *Night of the Living Dead*, only with ghosts instead of zombies. Zombies are instinctual. The ghosts knew exactly what they were doing. That, to me, was a hell of a lot scarier.

Remember *Titanic*? (Yeah, my dad's kicking himself over missing the boat—ha ha—on getting that idea before Cameron did.) I didn't understand why Leo was so whiny about how cold the water was. It wasn't colder than ice, right?

Wrong, moron. I went to a *Titanic* exhibit (about the actual historical event) sometime after the movie where they had water that was colder than freezing, because the ocean doesn't freeze, and I stuck my hand in it for a few seconds and nearly burst into tears because I finally understood just how fucking impossibly cold it had been for those people. (Not Leo. The real *Titanic* passengers.)

So now, when Solange started to scream, I had a sense of just how cold the ghosts felt, all over her.

I don't know if that itself could have killed her, because they obviously had other plans. They dragged at her until she started—disappearing. They were filtering her, taking her to whatever place it is they go when they blink away. Only, to my understanding, only ghosts could go there. Not living, breathing, corporeal people.

Apparently I'd been wrong, wrong, wrong.

I got the sense it was like being scraped through a razor-sharp screen.

The sounds Solange was making churned my stomach. Part of me wanted to turn away. Part of me wanted to stop this from happening. But part of me knew what she'd done, and I accepted that ghosts take care of their own, and it wasn't entirely my battle to fight anymore.

So I clenched the medallion in my hand until the symbol was etched into my palm, and I let it happen.

At first it was slow, excruciating, but at the very end all the ghosts started winking away, too, into that place, and the faster they disappeared, the hotter the room became. Rudy had said that the reason ghosts are cold, or the room gets cold, is because ghosts are sucking out the energy in order to manifest. Well, when they went, the opposite was bound to happen, right?

Energy came back.

And when a shitload of them went away all at the same time...

The *boom* knocked me off my feet. I skidded backwards just like the medallion had skidded to me, except there was nobody there to pick me up. Bruised and disoriented, I scrambled to my feet for the umpteenth time that night. Solange, and all the ghosts, were gone.

It was oddly breezy.

That's when I realized the solarium's glass roof, which had blown out along with the walls, was coming crashing back down.

I ducked and ran for the now-damaged French doors. Wishing *I* was wearing a hoodie, I hunched away from the rain of glass, noticing as I went that Bridget was gone.

Unfortunately, the interior of the hotel wasn't the safe haven it had always been for me. Because the backlash of energy had set it on fire. Not just the lobby. The entire damn hotel.

Boom and poof.

God*dammit*.

TWENTY-SIX

IT WAS JUST my luck that I'd be hauled out of the burning wreckage of the Ballington not by a ripped fire-fighter who would easily break down my defenses and convince me to bear his children, but by a middle-aged balding firefighter who, while still in excellent shape (wouldn't he have to be?), apparently saw me as a daughter figure.

And the EMT who wrapped me in a blanket and slapped an oxygen mask on my face was cute and all, but I didn't go for girls.

Sitting on the bumper of the ambulance, all I wanted to do was close my eyes and make everything go away.

I couldn't. I watched. I had to.

So this was it. Pffft. The last year of my life, everything I'd worked for, gone.

No. That hollow aching pit beneath my generous breast forced me to acknowledge that it was more than that.

That beautiful hotel, the stately graceful Ballington, all its history, disintegrating before my eyes. There was some-thing compelling, intoxicating, about the flames that lapped at the walls like a demented demon tongue. (Daddy, if you ever go into horror films, have I got a metaphor for you. On second thought, no, that was a crappy metaphor.) I touched my face, winced. If my eyebrows hadn't already been singed off, they'd be close to it now; even from across the street I sweated from the rolling waves of heat. I shrugged off the blanket.

The air stank of a campfire from Hell.

Also, Rudy was going to *kill* me. All his equipment had been inside.

My lungs were killing me. I'd've given anything not to have to breathe for a week. The oxygen was sweet and cool, though, and hey, people shell out good money at The Oxygen Bar for the privilege.

I thought I'd come to terms with betrayal—Eden, Chris, even Ned—but the revelation of Solange stripped me down to the bone. She'd never been my friend, and maybe that's what hurt the most. That she'd used me from the start, never intended for me to be anything but a tool to get what she really wanted.

Hell, I'd had so-called friends do that to me all my life, to get to my father or one of his actors or whatever. But Solange was the first one I'd never caught. Whom I'd trusted, blindly and stupidly in my own desperate need for belonging, from Day One.

Idiot.

And alone. Again. Except for a mute six-year-old who would have burrowed onto my lap if she could.

Janie had chosen to move on now that the hotel was gone. She'd stayed only because of her happy times there. Sam and Tabitha hadn't said goodbye completely, but they were going off by themselves somewhere for a while, to rekindle their relationship. They had decades of hurt to work through, so I wished them well. They'd be back, because Tabitha wanted me to find her son.

I missed them all.

Now I finally understood the real reason Otter had told me to find Tabitha. He'd told me to seek her out, not that she knew who was responsible for the missing ghosts. No, my story was too similar to hers: I had a secret, my friends had abandoned me, and the person I trusted most would betray me. Too bad I hadn't clued in until after the fact.

Asia suddenly materialized at my side.

"Holy crap!" A half laugh, half sob hitched out of me. Okay, not totally alone. Although I wasn't sure this was exactly better.

Asia and I weren't exactly BFFs, but at least she was someone to talk to. When she listened.

Plus, it meant that Solange hadn't won.

She'd taken Aaron and Marla and Curtis, and a few others, but she hadn't gotten Janie or Sam or Tabitha or Asia; she hadn't gotten Marilyn or any of the other ghosts. Hah! Take that!

A part of me was kind of bummed I hadn't found out where her hidden treasure was. It would have given me every level of smugness to say "neener neener" when I turned the money over to the police.

"Where've you been?" I asked.

"I don't know!" Asia seemed strangely excited by her own ignorance. "I just sort of...went away. It was like this nifty defense mechanism to get away. I mean, Janie had said something about that ability, but I hadn't really been paying attention, so I didn't know I could do it."

Sigh. I'd have to find her another ghostly mentor to explain the ins and outs of spirithood. Maybe Marilyn wouldn't mind a protégé for a while?

"Good thing I did, too, otherwise Solange might've gotten me," Asia went on.

"Why didn't you get sucked in at the beginning?" I wondered.

"I think she didn't know I was there."

It dawned on me that with everything going on, I'd never told Solange about Asia.

"So now it's just you and me, babe!" She held out her fist, expected me to bump it.

I stared at her.

"Oh, sorry." She dropped her hand.

"Everything okay here, hon?" the EMT asked. She was fit and trim, with black hair and dusky skin. Her eyes were so dark, I almost couldn't tell her irises from her pupils. "You looked like you blanked out for a moment."

"I'm fine," I said. "Just...thinking."

"It's a lot to deal with," she said. She reached out to pat my shoulder and I flinched away. "Don't be afraid to talk about it. Your doctor should be able to recommend someone."

"Oh, I already have a therapist," I said. "No prob there."

Come to think of it, another vacation at the "spa" might not be such a bad idea....

No. I mentally squared my shoulders. I wasn't running away this time. This was another chance to start over, and I wasn't going to waste time this time.

Of course, it would help if I knew what I wanted to do.

My heart wasn't in another hotel. Not yet, anyway. I needed to mourn the Ballington. But did I really want to take on another project like that? Was it worth the time and money? If I wanted to invest in a hotel, why didn't I just throw my lot in with a resort in Cancun and become a beach bum? I could teach surfing. Swim with ghost dolphins, if they existed. I wouldn't put it past dolphins to stick around for their afterlives.

My iPhone vibrated, letting me know I had a text. I fished it out of my pocket automatically, then stopped. I'd already left a message with Susie to tell my parents about the hotel and that I was fine. Anyone else who might be trying to contact me probably wasn't someone I wanted to talk to. (I'm looking at you, TMZ.)

But Asia leaned in and said "Ooh, who is it?" and let's face it, even if I don't always answer a call or text, I'm not very good at not at least checking to see who it's from.

My hand shook. Maybe not the last person I expected, but close.

TWENTY-SEVEN

BRIDGET'S MESSAGE said she was around the corner and needed to talk to me.

She'd made it out alive. I'd thought she had, in a vague, back-of-the-mind sense. It was strange to feel glad about that, after all the animosity I'd felt from her—or maybe thought I'd felt from her.

I'd been wrong about a lot.

I texted her back that I'd be there as soon as I could. I slid my phone back into my pocket and glanced around. The fire still roared and gnawed hunks out of my hotel, keeping the firefighters occupied. The EMT had her head bent, scribbling on a clipboard.

I eased the oxygen mask off my face. The stench of burning hopes and dreams assaulted me. Blinking away tears (the smoke and ash, you know), I slipped away.

I knew the cross street Bridget mentioned, a few blocks into the neighborhood behind the hotel. The air was appreciably cooler there, the darkness muddy from the red glow and haze of ashes.

She glanced to my right, then down, and I realized for the first time that she could see Asia and Maggie.

How could I ever believed Solange could communicate with spirits? She hadn't been that good an actress. I'd just been that good a sucker. I'd needed a friend that badly.

"Nikki," Bridget said, and for a moment I thought she was going to hug me. "I'm so sorry about Marla and Curtis and the others."

"Not about Solange?" I asked.

Her lips thinned. A dark bruise stood out on her temple, a shadow against her fair skin.

"I owe you an explanation," she said. "I was tasked to keep an eye on Solange."

Huh? "Tasked by whom?"

She moved her hand, not quite a dismissive gesture. "We're a group of...well, 'psychics' is probably the easiest term. We all have some sort of paranormal, supranormal power."

"Witches?"

"Various religions, actually."

I scowled. My forehead hurt when I did, and when I touched it, the skin was hot. I bet it looked like I had a wicked sunburn. "Whatever. So the boss of the group sent you—why?"

"What we do is try to keep things on an even keel, psychically and magically speaking. We sensed Solange was gathering power. Dark power. We needed to find out why and, if possible, I was to stop her before she did anything damaging."

"She was gathering power by exorcising the ghosts," I said. "So that was like a disturbance in the Force?"

Her lips twitched. "Actually, that's not far off. At first, though, I wasn't sure what she was doing and, I'm afraid, I thought you were part of it. I thought you were working together."

Oh. Oh! So that's why she'd always been so cold to me. I hadn't misread that. "What clued you in?"

"When she made the tisane for you," she said. "I knew it was to block your ability, and that didn't make sense."

"Why didn't you tell me then?"

"I still couldn't be completely sure you weren't involved." She shook her head. "I knew she was using you to get at the ghosts, but I didn't know if you were finding them for her."

"You could've asked," I muttered.

Now she did smile. "I suppose I could have, but I couldn't risk blowing my cover." She sobered. "I knew for sure when you called the store tonight and told me I was the person you suspected."

I vaguely remembered that, when I was brain-fogged from the drug. "I thought you were Solange."

"I figured as much. I could tell you were drugged, so I got here as fast as I could. I'm sorry everything got as far as it did. And if it hadn't been for you, she would've raised her partner from the dead and all hell would have broken loose."

"Literally?" Damn!

"Not exactly, but close enough. So, thank you. You did a great job, and, well, I've been authorized to invite you to join us."

"You want *me* to join your group of psychic defenders of the paranormal realm."

"Yes," she said. "We could really use someone like you—someone with your natural abilities."

Woah. Wow. Talk about tempting. It would certainly be a refreshing change of pace, and maybe I could teach surfing on the side. The biggest plus was that I wouldn't have to hide who I am, what I can do. I could talk to ghosts and nobody would look at me funny.

Acceptance. They were my people.

I opened my mouth to say yes.

What came out was, "You know, thanks for the offer, but I'm going to have to pass."

We both blinked in surprise. Actually, Asia did, too. Hard to say which of us was more gobsmacked.

"Maybe...maybe after I pull my head together," I clarified. "Right now, I've got a lot of shit to work through."

The offer was so, so tempting—but for all the wrong reasons. It would just be another way to escape the real problem. I didn't want to be alone. I'd never really been alone, not for long; I'd always found ways to surround myself with people again.

The Universe had just shown me that I had crappy luck with that—and now the Universe had taken most of them away again.

There were always going to be times when I'd be alone. I had to be okay with that. I had to figure out how to be alone, and who I was when I was alone.

Damn. Guess I don't need my therapist anymore. Talk about a breakthrough.

Although I'd probably need my therapist to get me *through* the alone part.

"...Oh," Bridget said. She didn't seem to know how to take that.

"Yeah, I know," I said. "I just shocked the hell out of me, too."

She fidgeted with the leather strap of her messenger bag. "Well," she said finally, "you've got my number. You know how to find us."

I nodded. "And if you need anything, let me know."

"Same here. Be well and be safe, Nikki Elizabeth Ashburne."

I felt a ripple of something deep in her words, that they weren't just a platitude but carried with them some sort of power. Or maybe I was still in shock, or maybe I just wanted to believe. Hard to say. But if there are ghosts, and weird evil voodoo juju, why not this? Why not anything?

"I can't believe you just did that," Asia said as Bridget walked away into the night.

"Stick around, I'm full of surprises," I said. I started walking back myself.

My phone rang. Jeez, I was just Miss Popularity all of a sudden.

"Hey, Donny," I said. "My hotel is burning down. Why aren't you here?"

"I know," he said. "Jesus, Nikki, that's awful. I left once I saw you were okay, because there's no way I'm going to stalk you at a time like this."

"And that's why you'll never really make it as a paparazzi," I said.

"I'm beginning to accept that sad reality," he said. "What happened? And how're you doing?"

He asked like he really meant it.

"I'll survive," I said, and didn't elaborate because my jaw clenched up and I knew if I did, I'd start to lose it.

Donny's voice was very quiet. "Do you need anything?"

I thought about asking him for a ride. I was pretty sure my Mini and my van were both beyond help. They were parked in the alley, and were probably *melted* in the alley by this point.

I thought about what I'd said to Bridget.

"No," I said. "I'll be fine."

I'd been planning on calling my father, on moving back in until I figured out where to go next. And, honestly, it wouldn't hurt to make the mansion a home base for a little while.

Not tonight, though. Tonight I needed a shower and a bed.

The Roosevelt was five minutes away. I'd call a Lyft.

I walked away from the fire and the mass of people that had crowded the area to watch. They didn't spare me a second glance, which was just fine with me.

SHADED

~

Turn the page for a special sneak preview
of the second Nikki Ashburn novel,
Shaded.

~

ONE

SO HERE'S SOMETHING I'VE learned: yelling at ghosts doesn't make them go away.

Nor does hissing at them between clenched teeth, which was really more what I was doing right now.

My name is Nikki Ashburne, and whether I like it or not, I see dead people.

Wait. Am I allowed to quote the movie tagline? You'd think growing up with a Hollywood-mega-producer father would have meant I'd have learned this by now. Let me start over.

Yes, I'm *that* Nikki Ashburne, former famous party girl (the kind who gets paid to appear). Then my beloved grandmother died and in an attempt to muffle my grief, I accidentally OD'd. Yeah, I'm one of those special people who tries drugs *once* and royally screws it up. I died briefly myself, and when I woke up, I could see ghosts. As in, my permanently dead grandmother was sitting on the end of my very expensive hospital room bed, and she slapped me and told me I was an idiot.

She was not the ghost I was currently hissing at. After

dispensing her wisdom, my grandmother had headed off to the great beyond, a decision that I've had to come to emotional terms with. The ghost in front of me now was Asia McBride.

Asia had been an up-and-coming It Girl, following the usual pattern; she'd starred in a kids' TV show, cut a single, started working the party circuit, got lined up for a reality show. She wasn't someone I hadn't really been friends with when we were both alive. But ghosts stick around because there's something here they prefer, or they're too scared to move on, or they just want to stay, and Asia has decided we're BFFs and now I can't get rid of her.

She was currently upset because she'd just learned that ghosts can't change their clothes—they're stuck in what they were wearing when they died. (No wonder the cliché is floating sheets. How many people die in bed? How many of those people are naked at the time?) Asia was wearing super-cute Herve Leger cap-sleeved bandage dress in a shade of teal that set off her tawny, freckle-dusted skin perfectly, and to-die-for strappy copper Jimmy Choos, but both were soon to be *so* last year's fashions.

Even though Asia is twenty-one and I'm twenty-four, I felt like her mother, because she kept asking "But *why*?" I didn't know *why* ghosts couldn't change clothes, any more than my own mother had known *why* kale was good for you so just eat it, or *why* I couldn't have a ring-tailed lemur for my fifth birthday.

For that matter, I also didn't know *why*, when Asia died at a beach party when she fell into the Jacuzzi and hit her head, she wasn't dripping everywhere. Life may not be fair, but maybe the afterlife is?

All I knew was, I was there when she died, so she'd latched on to me, and right now I was coming very close to saying "Because I said so!" which was a rather horrifying prospect.

Then my perfectly coiffed, *I must look much too young to have a daughter in her twenties* mother walked into the room with her three-olive martini, her heavy gold bracelets clunking against each other, and said, "There you are. Who are you talking to?"

I fumbled to come up with a response that didn't include an explanation about the seeing-ghosts thing. Very few people knew. When I told my baby brother, Ned, he didn't take it well at all. He decided I was lying and trying to get attention, and hadn't really spoken to me since.

I mumbled something about lines from a script. There were definite benefits to moving back in to my parents' ridiculously palatial Brentwood mansion, but having my mother randomly appear around the corner was not my favorite part of the day. The only plus in the situation was that Asia had stopped complaining. She was terrified of my mother. I didn't blame her.

I was staying at the mansion not because it had its own planetarium (a great place to neck with boyfriends back when I was in high school), but because I was between homes at the moment. I'd been living in, and restoring, a haunted, late-1920s Art Deco hotel, from which I'd been running ghost tours of Hollywood (with some of the ghosts' assistance). After it burned down (long story), I'd taken up residence at a suite in the Roosevelt Hotel—not haunted, as rumor had it, by the ghost of Marilyn Monroe, but by the ghost of a Marilyn Monroe *impersonator*, who's a friend of mine—but that shit ain't cheap. So I came home for a little while.

I'd been hanging out in the mansion's library, which looked like one of those massive medieval church libraries, except without the books chained up to keep them from being stolen. (We had a high-tech security system to prevent thieves, paparazzi, wanna-be actors, and your garden variety obsessive types.) Two stories high, with a wheeled wooden ladder hooked to a brass bar around the top. When we were little, Ned would climb the ladder and I would push it around while he laughed gleefully. Happy times.

It was all dark wood and a beamed ceiling and heavy, solid furniture, and a huge stone fireplace in which a sweetly smoky fire crackled and popped. The evening was overcast, chilly for Southern California.

I liked this room because it felt old, historic, and I'd discovered a love for that in the last year or so. Maybe I'd always felt it, but hadn't been able to put a name to it. When I was younger, I'd preferred to spent time in Grandma Rosa's house—she'd lived in the guest house on the estate—but I'd also liked this room a lot.

It was full of books nobody read, but were important to have. Daddy spent his time reading scripts and trade news, and my mother read fashion magazines and kept tabs on the latest gossip via the Internet. I had an iPad Mini with various book and magazine apps on it, for the rare moments I had time to read anything. Goodness knew I'd spent a year reading about ghosts and then about restoring historic buildings. I probably needed to lose myself in a taut thriller or fluffy romance.

"Well," my mother said, "if you want to get back into acting, you have our support, of course." I'd had small parts in a few of my father's movies. Nothing to write home about. "Anyway, I just wanted to let you know we're having a family dinner tonight."

My mother fits pretty much every cliché of a rich Hollywood wife. She devoted her life to supporting my father, handling everything about the house and their social life so he could focus on his work. That much I appreciated, because I adore my father. She threw splendid parties, invited all the right people, charmed them. She did just enough charity work to look good without spending so much time on it that she neglected her other duties.

And she worked hard to be the epitome of the perfect spouse. The carefully apportioned doses of Botox kept her skin smooth but not mask-tight; the most expensive lotions and creams kept it soft; the perfect level of makeup kept her looking polished but not obviously painted. Her blond hair was expensively colored and cut every three weeks in the salon here in the mansion by an exclusive stylist.

She despairs of me, because I just can't be bothered with all of that anymore. I ditched my extensions and have my own blond hair in an unfashionble (but terribly cute, if I say so myself) 1920s-ish bob, and I'm more likely to dress for stylish comfort than to show off the latest fashions. (Another reason why I didn't sympathize with Asia's predicament.) Right now I had on jeans, black-and-white checked Vans, and a light-knit red sweater with a knitted black wrap thrown over it.

"I can't," I said automatically, because a family dinner sounded on par with getting a Brazilian without a Xanax and Vicodin first. "I have plans."

"What plans?"

My mother is not stupid, and I'm not the greatest liar. Thankfully I had a plausible explanation, if untrue. "I have an appointment to see some rentals with my Realtor."

"Surely that can wait," my mother said, with a sigh that encompassed all the ways I'd disappointed her. "We have something we need to discuss with you and Ned."

That sounded worse. That sounded like getting a

Brazilian without Xanax and Vicodin while being hit on by the aesthetician.

I was groping for a suitable comeback excuse when my phone whooshed to let me know I had a text.

Rudy's message was straight to the point: "Need yr help. Galleria."

"My Realtor," I blithely lied, wagging my phone. "If I don't check this place out ASAP, it'll be gone. You know what rentals are like right now."

My mother had no clue, but she'd never admit it.

Before she could respond, a second text made a whooshing noise on my phone: "You owe me."

"See? Super important," I said, texting back that I'd meet him in an hour, because LA traffic, ugh. "We can reschedule, right? Have Susie text me and I'll put it in my calendar." Susie was my mother's assistant, and sometimes we ended up communicating through her.

Yes, I know my life is weird.

I didn't know it was about to get a lot weirder.

ACKNOWLEDGMENTS

Thank you to Kristine Kathryn Rusch and Kerrie L. Hughes for buying Nikki short stories for volumes of Fiction River, allowing me to explore the background of Nikki's world, and to the Uncollected Anthology project for inspiring me to write even more Nikki stories.

Thank you to Thorn Coyle and Leah Cutter, who encouraged me and propped me up during the final week of my arduous rearranging and tying all the pieces together, and for not letting me run away from the computer when my ass needed to be planted firmly in the chair.

Thank you to my first reader, Leslie Claire Walker, who ensured the book actually made sense, and my dauntless copyeditor, Colleen Kuehne, who caught all the embarrassing mistakes. If anything embarrassing remains, it's not their fault. (It's Nikki's fault. When in doubt, blame Nikki.)

Thank you to amazing cover artist Melody Simmons, who visually created the Nikki in my head, which was no small feat. Just look at that attitude!

Thank you to my beloved, Ken, who believed in this book well before I did, and who believes in me always even when I don't believe in myself. (His response to this will probably be "Well, *duh*. You're awesome." No, *you're* awesome, with a side of awesomesauce, and I love you.)

I really, honestly, truly would never have finished this one without all of you.

ABOUT THE AUTHOR

Called "one of the best writers working today" by best-selling author Dean Wesley Smith, Dayle A. Dermatis is the author or coauthor of many novels and more than a hundred short stories in multiple genres, including urban fantasy novel *Ghosted* and its forthcoming sequels, *Shaded* and *Spectered*. She is a founding member of the Uncollected Anthology project, and her short fiction has been lauded in year's best anthologies in erotica, mystery, and horror.

She lives in a book- and cat-filled historic English-style cottage in the wild greenscapes of the Pacific Northwest. In her spare time she follows Styx around the country and travels the world, which inspires her writing.

To find out where she's wandered off to (and to get free fiction!), check out DayleDermatis.com.

For more information:
www.dayledermatis.com

BE THE FIRST TO KNOW!

SIGN UP for Dayle A. Dermatis's newsletter for *free* fiction every month, plus the latest news, releases, and more.

Click here or sign up at DayleDermatis.com.

"One of the best writers working today."
– *USA Today* bestselling author Dean Wesley Smith

Written on the Coast

a collection of 13 fantasy and science fiction stories

Available now in print and e-book formats

89526805R00148

Made in the USA
Columbia, SC
22 February 2018